What Stays in Vegas

Beth Labonte

Cover illustration by Linda Wyatt
Cover design by Kevin Labonte

Originally published e-book, May 2011
First paperback edition, March 2013

ISBN-13: 978-1461154471
ISBN: 1461154472

Visit my website at www.bethlabonte.com

1

I peeled my eyes away from the rain coming down in sheets across my windshield and glanced at the clock on the dashboard. 2:57 p.m.

"There's no way," I said out loud. "There's no *effing* - ahh!"

A Hummer-driving maniac came out of nowhere and narrowly missed my left fender as they cut into the lane in front of me.

"Jerk!" I yelled. "The grocery store gonna close soon?"

I took a deep breath and with one hand reached over to reposition the box of engineering plans sitting on my passenger seat. This was total insanity.

Not only was this one of the worst rain storms that I've ever driven through in my life, but I also had a sore throat that every time I swallowed felt like Johnny Depp was swashbuckling his way out of my epiglottis.

The afternoon had started off relatively okay. I had just settled in at my desk with a nice hot cup of tea with honey, when the annoying little leprechaun's footsteps came to a halt outside my cubicle. Apparently there was a life or death situation involving these plans getting up to Dover, New Hampshire before the town hall closed at 3:30 p.m. Otherwise, another one of our precious Jiggly Kitty strip joints might not get built.

No, that's not true. It would still get built, it just might be delayed a couple of months. And in the larger scheme of things, it is much better to risk your administrative assistant's life than to cost your creepy client a few months income. Besides, it was 1:53 p.m. when I left, which, according to the leprechaun, is plenty of time to get somewhere in the middle of a typhoon. Especially when you're driving 30 mph on the highway.

My posture had deteriorated into that of an eighty-five year old nursing home patient. My back was tense and my fingers, the ones that hadn't loosened their grip on the steering wheel in over an hour, were beginning to cramp up. And yet throughout all of this, there were still people driving like absolute lunatics.

Just because they drive these monstrous vehicles -

The sound of my ringing cell phone jolted me from my internal rant.

Keith Burns. The leprechaun.

Don't get me wrong, I'm not a racist towards the Irish or anything. I don't even know if Keith is Irish. I'm sure as hell not involved enough in his personal life to know that kind of information. I call him a leprechaun simply because he is a bouncy, spritely, little thing with way too much enthusiasm for civil engineering. If there were ever anybody cut out for scampering around at the end of rainbows, it was this guy.

"Hello?" I said, trying to keep the car steady while holding my cell.

"Tessa, hey," said Keith. I could barely hear him over the rain. "Whereabouts are you?"

Whereabouts am I? On a fucking merry-go-round. Where do you think I am?

"Just outside Lowell," I said instead, glancing at a road sign. "About a half hour from Dover, why?"

"Ok, cool. Look, I just got a call from the client and we don't need those plans delivered after all. So you can just go ahead and come back to the office."

As his words sank in, so did my car. I'd suddenly become submerged by some kind of tidal wave, and my wipers were struggling to keep up.

Oh God, I'm actually going to die while on the phone with the leprechaun.

For a split second I couldn't see a thing. For a split second I was lost in a sea of dirty flood water and anger. Rising anger.

"Oh," I said. "Um, you realize that I've been driving for an hour in some pretty bad weather, right?" I forced a laugh that felt like sandpaper in my throat.

"Yeah, cool," he said, not listening to me. "So just head on back. I've got a few proposals for you to type up. Tessa? You there?"

Proposals? But it's already 3:00 p.m. By the time I get back...

"Yeah, I'm here. The rain is just really ba - "

"Hello?"

"YES! I'm here! I just have a pretty sore - "

"Tessa?"

"I FEEL LIKE SHIT, OK?!" I used my throat's last ounce of strength to get my point across. But there was nothing but dead air at the other end - which, in retrospect, was probably a good thing. Still, I whipped my cell phone onto the floorboard and violently pulled off at the next exit.

I came to a stop at the bottom of the ramp and glanced into my rearview mirror just in time to watch myself get rear-ended by an olive green Hummer. My airbag punched me in the face, just as the back window of my Jeep popped open and icy pellets of hail gusted in- soaking me, soaking the precious plans, soaking everything.

Cursing the world, I pulled to the side of the road to exchange insurance information. None of this should have surprised me though. This day just about summed up my life.

No wonder I wanted out.

2

I've wanted out since day one. Not just day one of this job, but day one of every crappy job that has come before it. Pretty much ever since the day I unintentionally landed myself a career as an administrative "professional." Call me what you like, what I really am is a glorified secretary.

I've built up a tolerance to it, for the most part. I've come to tolerate the endless filing, the constant interruptions, the fact that there is a day in April dedicated to the appreciation of me. You know you're in a dead-end job when you get a holiday forcing people to appreciate you. The obligatory flowers that turn up on our desks when the big day arrives are always nice. Obligatory flowers are better than no flowers at all, though I'd prefer the extra fifty bucks in my paycheck if I had a choice. But yeah, I don't have a choice.

My problem is not that I couldn't continue to do this job day in and day out for the rest of my life. I most certainly could. I could do this job with my hands tied behind my back and my head in a paper bag. Some Mondays I've been tempted to do this job with my head in a plastic bag. But let's not get morbid.

My point is that I work in a nice office and get along with most of my coworkers. I do not have to clean toilets, make change, or slice deli meats. Many times I'm able to sneak an extra twenty minutes into my lunch hour. My cubicle is spacious and I get two weeks for vacation. There are some sickos out there who might even be envious.

My problem lies in the fact that if I, Tessa Golden, were to suddenly find myself eighty years old, lying on my death bed and looking back upon my life, would I find anything there to be proud of? Or would I see nothing but filing and typing and paper cuts? What runs shivers down my spine is that even after I am gone, the filing will continue to pile up, and a new administrative assistant will be along to continue the cycle. It will be as if I never existed.

I will never have made my mark on the world. The pointlessness of it all is not what dreams are made of. It is certainly not what *my* dreams are made of. Or *were* made of. I've lost track these days.

One thing making it particularly hard to keep track of anything at the moment was Nick Trask - tall, dark, and dripping wet - smiling at me from the driver's seat of his pickup. My Jeep ended up having to be towed, so I called Nick to come and get me. He's my best friend from work, and before you make any assumptions about my feelings for him, let me just confirm that they are all correct.

"Did Keith go home yet?" I asked. I turned up the heat and blasted my face with the most wonderful feeling hot air.

"Nah," said Nick. "He was still bouncing around when I left. We'll sneak you in the back. You can hang out in my office until I finish up, then I'll take you home."

The rain was coming down just as bad as it had been before, but here in Nick's truck it wasn't scary or annoying at all. It was kind of cozy. I turned up the radio and sank back into my seat.

Nick was single when we met during my early days at Flamhauser-Geist, and we had a good three years to fall madly in love with each other. At least I held up my end of the bargain. But for Nick, at least as far as I know, it never happened. We've been to countless drunken Christmas parties together, movies, lunches - yet he never made a move. At one point I began to wonder if he was gay, except for the fact that he dated plenty of other girls. Perhaps he just valued our friendship more than I did, or maybe he simply found me repulsive.

All I know is that one day, about a year ago, Nick returned from a Caribbean cruise a married man. He had met this girl on board, a foreclosure attorney, and he married her as soon as the boat docked in Florida. I cried myself to sleep for a week before I began to turn my anger at Nick into bitterness towards his new wife, Megan. She was pretty, therefore she had to be a bitch. She was super nice to everybody, therefore she was definitely a phony. If he were married to *me* he would never work late. She must treat him just terribly at home. All those smiling photographs in his office? Those were just for show.

Okay, okay, I'm not that delusional. I know that he's probably deliriously happy, goes home each night to his lingerie clad wife, and they make love on a bed of rose petals and puppies. This is just how I cope. The fact of the matter is that Nick Trask is smart, hot, and completely unattainable. He is the bane of my office existence, and married or not, he is the only thing that gets me into the office each morning.

We pulled into the parking lot and went up the back staircase to Nick's office. I sat down in his client chair while he grabbed a red pencil and went to work scribbling on some plans. Nick is an engineer, but he's more "one of us" than "one of them." By that I mean he can schmooze with clients just as well as anyone in upper management, but he can also still appreciate a good article from *The Onion.* His sense of humor has stayed in tact.

"So, how's married life going?" I asked, hoping to sound casual.

"It's, uh, you know, it's great," said Nick. He grabbed an eraser out of his drawer and removed a few red scribbles without looking up at me.

"Great like the way I say filing is great? Or great like 'Hey there's a baby on the way!'?"

Nick looked up at me silently for a second, then arched an eyebrow. "There's definitely no baby on the way. Not at this rate."

Not at this rate? What did that mean? My vision of rose petals and puppies suddenly went poof.

"What are you talking about?" I asked.

"You know, we just don't have much - "

Just as I was about to hear potentially life-changing news about the love of my life's marital status, my stupid boss, Tom Skeeter, had to poke his head through the door.

"Tessa! I thought I might find you here," said Tom. "Would you mind swinging by my office when you get a second?"

"Sure," I said. I was always swinging into people's offices. One day I want to literally swing in from a chandelier, just for the hell of it. I stood up to walk back with him, but by the time I got into the hallway he was already long gone. Nobody at Flamhauser-Geist walked at normal speeds.

"Be right back," I said to Nick.

As I walked into Tom's office I saw that the rain had finally started to clear. It was December and I should probably have just been grateful that it wasn't snowing. Either way it was cold and disgusting outside. If I didn't have family here in Massachusetts I would have left for a warmer climate a long time ago. Scraping my windshield each winter morning with ice crystals stinging my face and snow soaking into my heels is pretty much hell on earth, except that Hell is much warmer. And certainly administrative assisting cannot possibly be as depressing if your office is overlooking West Palm Beach, rather than the gloriously scenic MBTA commuter rail tracks.

Speaking of which, those tracks taunt me. They make me think of where I could go if I were on one of those trains. It's all very silly as I know exactly where that train goes. Boston. And what would I do in Boston that is different from what I do here? Most likely I would work at another civil engineering company as another administrative assistant. Perhaps I would work in a high rise building, or for a bigger and more important firm. I would definitely spend more of my paycheck on lunchtime shopping. So maybe I am better off where I am.

"Have a seat," said Tom, who had already managed to get back to his desk and start typing an email. The man could type emails in his sleep. I pushed aside a set of plans and sat myself down on the leather couch, studying the top of his curly gray head as I waited. I could literally tell by his hair how much energy he had. Each curl was unusually perky that afternoon, as if they had personally taken a sip from the bucket sized cup of coffee on his desk.

With a few more brisk taps to his keyboard Tom sent off his email and leaned back in his chair. It was a little hard to take him seriously with the framed picture of the very first built Jiggly Kitty strip club hanging on the wall behind his head, but I tried my best.

"So," he said, "do you remember Kendra Stoltz? Branch Manager out in our Las Vegas office? I think you met her at the Christmas party."

Ah, the Flamhauser-Geist Holiday Gala. This is when all four branches converge on a hotel ballroom dressed in their finest, get totally shitty from the all-night open bar, and are kindly asked by hotel management to find themselves another venue next year.

I remembered the night quite clearly. Nick and Megan were slow dancing to *Wonderful Tonight*, and I could tell that Nick was singing the lyrics into her ear. Totally vomit-worthy. I stood by the bar downing a gin and tonic, while some freakazoid from Las Vegas tried to make conversation. He said his name was Todd Stoltz and that he had a Twister board upstairs in his room. Clothing optional. At that point I excused myself and hurried off to the ladies room where I noticed a blonde kneeling in front of a toilet trying not to vomit.

"Are you alright?" I called over to her from the sinks. She sniffed and wiped her mouth with about three hundred squares of toilet paper.

"Too...many...shots. Look, look what I did." She turned and jabbed at a bluish stain smack in the middle of her white dress. "My husband is so embarrassed."

"Oh I'm sure he won't even remember any of this tomorrow," I said. I pulled a travel sized stain removal stick out of my purse. "Come sit over here, we'll get that stain right out." I sat her down on the ladies room couch and rubbed some stain remover into her dress. It didn't exactly come out as I'd promised, but it did turn to a lighter shade of blue.

"Oh my God, I love you. You're the awesomest awesome person ever." She hiccupped and held out her hand. "I'm Kendra. Kendra Stoltz."

Stoltz. She had to be kidding me.

"Tessa," I said, shaking her hand and trying not to picture her husband upstairs playing a game of naked Twister with the housekeeper. "From the Massachusetts office."

"Jessica," she muttered, closing her eyes. "That's a pretty name."

"Actually it's - "

"Jessica," repeated Kendra. "You're my new best friend." She leaned over and gave me a drunken, sloppy, hug.

After that, I had helped her off the couch, walked her back to the ballroom, and never saw her again.

"I think I met her briefly in the ladies room," I said to Tom.

"Well, you must've made quite an impression. I got a call from her last night," he said. "Her assistant will be going on maternity leave and she needs somebody to fill her place. She's requested you, Tessa. Actually, she requested somebody named 'Jessica,' but I put two and two together." Tom smiled.

The words took several seconds to sink in. Las Vegas. Maternity leave. She requested Jessica. I was Jessica!

"You want me to go to Las Vegas?" I asked slowly. "You're serious?"

"Completely serious," said Tom. "It's a three month deal."

Despite the joy rising up inside of me and the desire to scream "Yes!" from the roof tops, I was slightly insulted that they would just hand me over for three months. Who would type their letters? Send their faxes? It is true that a monkey could do my job, but I didn't think there were any other monkeys so readily available.

"But, um, don't you guys need me here?" I asked.

"Tessa, don't think for a second that we're happy about losing you. But you know Kendra, she has a lot of pull around here." He pushed his glasses to the top of his head where they were instantly swallowed up by curls.

Kendra did have a lot of influence in the company. Perhaps I didn't mention that she is also the daughter of company President, Mr. Sean Flamhauser, owner of the very couch upon which I sat.

"It's just temporary anyway, and we can make do with Donna until you get back," said Tom.

Fifty-seven year old Donna Spang - when she wasn't outside smoking she was inside enveloped in a cloud of hairspray. So basically, the company just wasn't going to survive.

"It's a free trip to Vegas, Tessa. I would never stand in your way."

"I'm just shocked," I said. "I mean I only met Kendra for like ten minutes, and that was a *year* ago."

"Hey, whatever happened between you two in that ladies room, it worked." said Tom. "I requested a transfer to Vegas quite a few times and never got it."

"Oh no!" I said. "You wanted to leave us?"

"This was years ago, back when Donna was the only admin around here. Half the office probably put in for transfers." He gave me a wink. "But I guess I didn't have the right connections. Maybe I should have hung out more often in the ladies room."

"I'm thinking that would have landed you in jail, not Vegas."

I know that I called him stupid earlier, but I really love Tom. He has never spoken a single harsh word to me, and for the most part has always treated me like I actually have a brain. In return, I developed loads of respect for the guy, which is not something many people can say about their bosses. You might even say that I will miss him.

"So it's settled?" he asked. "You accept?"

"Of course I accept!" An icy rain was once again beating down on the window behind him. The weather was only going to get worse around here, but now it no longer mattered. I was going to Vegas.

We sat and talked for a few more minutes. Tom made a joke about how I shouldn't gamble away all my paychecks. I said something back about how I was sure I'd find other ways to spend my money in Vegas. Then I kind of wished I hadn't said that. Even with a sense of humor, there are things you regret saying to your boss. But he was cool about it, as usual. He told me I was to leave in early January, and that Flamhauser-Geist would be putting me up in one of those business hotel suites, all expenses paid. *Me* in a hotel suite on business. All expenses paid. It is a crazy world we live in.

A train full of commuters passed below Tom's window and tooted its horn. For once I did not wish to be on it, as Boston seemed rather dull after this unexpected turn of events.

3

This strange little hobby I have started when I was on the phone one morning with Jiggly Kitty tech support. Their web based document upload system hadn't been working, so I sat there on hold for at least half an hour and I began bending a paperclip. Then I started bending two paperclips. By the time a human being came on the line, I had crafted a perfect little stick figure. And by the time I got off the call, the little stick figure had a little desk and a little chair, all made out of paperclips, and I was well on my way to fashioning him a little computer. For Nick's birthday I made him a paperclip man holding a paperclip dish - then I filled it with paperclips. I considered filling it with staples or thumbtacks, just for the irony, but birthdays are not always the right time for irony.

My office supply sculptures have become more and more intricate over the past year. I have about fifteen of them spread out around my cubicle right now, and I've branched out to include binder clips, erasers, pushpins, and whatever other supplies I can get my hands on. I was warned once by Margaret Sherman, head of Human Resources and a serious pain in my ass, about stealing office supplies. But as soon as I showed her that all the supplies were in fact still in my cubicle, she backed off. I think it was mainly because she just didn't *get* it. The woman is seriously lacking in creativity. If she needed a binder clip she would easily disassemble my Eiffel Tower without even batting an eye. I skipped lunch to work on that tower, it's no joke.

I punched 212 into my phone and waited for Kara to answer. Kara Kelley is our receptionist and pretty much my only female friend in the office. What can I say? I just don't mesh very well with girls. But Kara's different. As soon as I found out that she owned a dog named Larry, I knew that we were meant to be friends. Me, Kara, Larry, and my goldfish...Barbara. It's not everyday that you find someone who shares your love of pets with human names.

"Hiya," answered Kara.

"You hoarding any boxes up there?" I asked.

"Did you just call me a whore?"

"*Hoarding* you moron! I need a few boxes to pack up my sculptures so Margaret doesn't ransack them the next time she needs an eraser."

"That bitch totally would," said Kara. "Though, you are kind of a freak with those office supplies, you know that right?" said Kara.

"You got the boxes or what?"

"Yeah, yeah. I'll be right over."

A couple of minutes later Kara popped around the corner carrying two empty boxes.

"I can't believe you're already leaving this weekend," she

said. She perched herself on my desk and kicked up one leg, then the other. "You nervous?"

Nervous? I'd been so busy packing and getting my Massachusetts life ready to go on hold for three months that I'd barely had time to think about it. But yeah, I suppose I was a little nervous. I mean, I didn't actually know anybody in Vegas. And I would be staying all by myself in a strange hotel. And what if my new coworkers didn't like me? I mean, it's no secret that I don't mesh well with girls, and my new boss is a girl, and...oh God, I was so nervous.

"Uh, no, not really," I lied. "It's just going to be such a great opportunity for me, you know? It'll be good to get away from this place for a while and maybe figure some stuff out." I gave her a meaningful look. Kara was the only other person in the world who knew about my feelings for Nick.

"So are you getting an expense account too?" she asked, kindly changing the subject.

I nodded.

"Holy crap." She shook her head and kicked my filing cabinet with her heel.

"But it's not like I can use it for anything I want," I said. "It's just for work related stuff. It's really not that great." I suddenly felt the need to downplay my good fortune. I mean, if it had been Kara instead of me who was being whisked away to Vegas, I would probably be in the ladies room in tears right now.

"Whatever," she said, making a rude gesture with her finger. "I'm so jealous of you that I might not even tell you the moronic thing Donna did this morning."

"No, please! Tell me!" I begged. "I'm going to be living three months without Donna Spang, don't deprive me of a few last memories."

"Well," said Kara. "She came in carrying a dozen hard boiled -"

Yet another juicy conversation was cut short as Tom walked in to grab something off my printer. We quieted the conversation down a bit and Kara acted as if she were just leaving to get the phone that had been ringing off the hook for the last five minutes. We would continue our conversation via email anyway. Eighty percent of our day was spent sending emails to each other. The other twenty percent was spent wondering how many of them were being read by the IT guy.

That afternoon, Kara and Nick took me out to TGI Friday's for a goodbye lunch where the three of us drank frozen margaritas bigger than our faces.

"There's nothing wrong with coming back to the office buzzed," Nick told us. "Trust me, the managers do it all the time."

I returned to my desk ready for a nap, but was instead faced with pages and pages of redlines from Keith. Redlines are when you hand something in that you typed up and your boss decides he wants everything to be different. Out comes the red pen, and your document is transformed into a bloodbath of scribbles and arrows, undecipherable to the untrained eye. Apparently leaving for Las Vegas wasn't a good enough reason for the leprechaun to stop bothering me, so I settled in front of my computer for the rest of the afternoon.

The last few hours ticked slowly away, until finally I was carrying my two cardboard boxes into Nick's office for safekeeping. As soon as I walked in, he stood up from his desk and wrapped his arms around me. He lifted me slightly off the ground.

"We'll see you in three months," he mumbled into my neck. Then he kissed me on the cheek.

"Three months, good sir," I said, then regretted it. Who says "good sir?" 19th century British shopkeepers, that's who. These are the reasons I'm still single.

Nick lowered me back to the ground and we stood there awkwardly for a few seconds, just kind of looking at each other.

"Well," I said, backing slowly towards the door. "I'll see ya soon." I gave him a little wave and left his office without looking back.

I figured he would just leave my sculptures in the box, but as I walked out to my car I could see him in the window already unpacking them along the sill. Late afternoon sun glinted off the metal arms and legs. I knew that I was only leaving for three months, but tears came to my eyes just the same.

Nick looked out into the parking lot and smiled when he spotted me. Then, I'll be damned - he blew me a kiss.

What on Earth has gotten into that boy?

I got into my car and started the engine. Whatever had gotten into him, I tell you this: if my plane crashes tomorrow, I will die a happy woman.

***

We had been in the air about two hours when I dozed off

to whichever Jarvis Brothers movie was being shown on my flight. I have never been on a flight that wasn't showing a Jarvis Brothers movie. You know what I'm talking about. They make these extremely dumb and unrealistic movies that cause you to feel dumber after you've watched them. This one involved two men running around in a horse costume fooling everybody into thinking they were a real horse. I mean even the veterinarian at the racetrack thought that they were a real horse. Truly awful, awful, stuff. I would've given anything for Nick or Kara to be sitting beside me, armed with a sarcastic commentary, but all I had was a middle aged man straight out of the Tommy Bahama catalog. He wasn't half bad looking, but he smelled like an alcoholic.

"Excuse me," I said, leaning across him to take a glass of red wine from the stewardess. I settled back in my seat, took a long sip, and closed my eyes. *Tessa Golden's Expense Account: 10:30 a.m. in-flight alcoholic beverage. Check.*

"So," said a voice next to me. "You traveling for business...or pleasure?"

I opened my eyes to find Tommy Bahama studying me with a disturbing amount of interest. I was actually pretty surprised he had gone a full two hours before speaking to me.

"Business," I said. "How about yourself?"

"A little of both. I'm going to Vegas to be a tooth model at a dental convention."

"A tooth model?" I asked, trying to appear politely interested. "What exactly does that involve?"

"Well," he said, "for a few hours I just have to lay in a chair with my mouth open and let a bunch of dentists admire my teeth." He shifted in his seat to face me, allowing me a full frontal view of his grill. He had a pretty nice set.

"Really?" I said. "How'd you manage that?"

"A close friend of mine is this hot shot cosmetic dentist out in California," he said smugly. "He does all my dental work for free."

"You fly to California every time you need dental work?" Sounded like bull shit to me.

"No, he comes out to Boston every so often to visit his family, so we do it then."

"Does he have an office out here? Or does he just do it in his living room?"

"Yeah, he's got an office out here." Tooth Model took a swig of his rum and Coke and checked his watch as if I was the one bothering him.

"Well, what about just regular cleanings?" I asked. I was starting to enjoy getting on this guy's nerves. "Does he do those too?"

"No, he doesn't. He's too busy to do regular cleanings. I have another guy for that." Tooth Model closed his eyes and jammed his seat back into the woman behind him. I looked around the plane trying to spot an air marshal with a taser, just in case things got weird.

"Sorry I asked," I muttered. We sat in awkward silence for about three minutes. Tooth Model let out a long sigh and swished his drink around his precious teeth.

"Well, how about you?" he asked, suddenly speaking to me again. "What kind of business are you in?"

"I work with engineers," I said. "We build Wal-Marts and gas stations and, uh, strip clubs." I took a long sip of my wine as I spoke the last part of that sentence.

"Strip clubs? Really?" Tooth Model sat up a little straighter in his seat. It figured that would catch his interest.

"Yeah," I said. "We have this big client called The Jiggly Kitty. What they try to do is instead of putting up new clubs and pissing off a lot of psycho housewives, they just buy up existing local clubs. Then they hire us to help with the remodel."

It's true. My bosses file zoning applications, go to town hearings, get their tires slashed, and are quite often told by angry women that we will burn in Hell. The citizens who are in support of The Jiggly Kitty would never show their faces at a public hearing, not when their wives are the ones leading the revolt.

"So you're an engineer?" asked Tooth Model.

"Nah," I said, a slight wave of shame coursing through me. "Just a secretary. I have a Bachelor's degree in Art, but I just kind of ended up, um, here instead." I looked out the window and imagined myself jumping out of it, down into the clouds.

"What the hell'd ya do that for?"

"Major in art? I don't know, I just loved it. I used to make stuff out of garbage. I would spend hours at flea markets just brows -"

"No, I mean why'd you end up a secretary?"

"Oh, I guess I just never figured out anything else to do. I mean, there isn't much of a market out there for trash sculptures."

While I was submersed in the carefree, indulgent, world of college, I spent my weekends in the studio or at flea markets hunting for materials. I never really thought about what I would do when it all came to an end. But after graduation the real world became much clearer and my mother's words came back to haunt me: *What the heck are you going to do with an art degree?*

Well, I took my first job as an elementary school art teacher but the little brats made me miserable.

Then I took my second job as an administrative assistant at an insurance agency just to make some money until I could figure things out. Unfortunately, the more time that passed, the more experience I gained as a secretary, making it harder for me to switch gears and look for a job in the art world. By the time I was hired by Flamhauser-Geist I realized that I had become rather good at administrative assisting. I was organized and efficient, I typed letters and made paperclip holders out of paperclips. Maybe it wasn't so bad.

"That's too bad," said Tooth Model. "You seem like a smart girl."

"Thanks," I said, giving him a genuinely appreciative smile. Maybe he wasn't as sleazy as I thought. Maybe -

"So, you want to join the mile high club?"

Maybe I was an excellent judge of character.

I put an immediate end to the conversation by plugging in my headphones and turning my attention back to the movie that was getting increasingly worse. That's about when I fell asleep. The thought that Tooth Model was trying to peer down my shirt was definitely a concern as I drifted off, but it was still better than letting that conversation continue for even another second.

4

I woke with a jolt to the voice of the captain announcing our descent into Las Vegas. Temperature: Eighty-seven degrees. Skies: Sunny. I sat up and looked over at Tooth Model who was trying to persuade the stewardess to bring him one more rum and Coke before we landed. He flashed her his million dollar grin. She didn't stand a chance.

I leaned forward and looked out at the blue sky, my ears popping slightly. Before I knew it, there was the Las Vegas strip, growing larger and larger every second. There was the Luxor, the Bellagio, the Mirage, and way down at the end, the Stratosphere! A light breeze on the back of my neck startled me and I banged my head into the glass. I turned to find Tooth Model's face about three inches away from mine. The pervert had unbuckled his seat belt and was practically kneeling on the floor next to me.

"That view gets me every time," he said, letting out a creepy whistle.

"Sir, *please*, we need everybody in their seats with their seat belts *on*," said the stewardess. She handed him what was probably his fifth rum and Coke and hurried off to her own seat at the back of the plane. Tooth Model swallowed the drink in two gulps.

"You don't get no reward for trying to be a friendly guy," he muttered, fastening his seat belt. He was pretty drunk and I wasn't too sure what he was talking about, but it didn't matter. In a few minutes I would be off the plane, and I was starting to get nervous.

I mentally planned out what I needed to do when I disembarked as this was the first time I had ever traveled alone. The first thing was to get my luggage, and then pick up the rental car that Flamhauser-Geist had reserved for me. Then came the worst part, finding my way to the Las Vegas Marriott Suites - my new home for the next three months. Driving in the city terrifies me. I have never once driven through Boston. And now I was in Las Vegas where there would be beautiful people in sports cars and limousines honking at me to get the hell out of the way as I gripped the steering wheel of my un-cool rental sedan.

I filed off the plane, watching with delight as Tooth Model headed in the direction of the restrooms while I took off the opposite way toward baggage claim. The airport was busy on a Saturday morning. Smiling people just starting their vacations criss-crossed paths with glum looking people waiting to head back home. I gloated to myself as I realized I had three whole months ahead of me before it would be my turn at the departure gate. I tried not to look too smug as I followed the signs and dodged the crowds. The sound of slot machines - slot machines at an airport! - rose above the sound of families shouting to each other, which rose above the sound of people shouting into their cell phones. I felt a bit lonely, having nobody to shout at myself. But I was soon distracted by the fifteen thousand identical black suitcases coming around the luggage carousel. I am proud to say, however, that mine was the only one sporting a neon pink Jiggly Kitty luggage tag, just one of the many items you can purchase in The Jiggly Kitty gift shop. Did I not mention that The Jiggly Kitty has a gift shop? Not only can you purchase a souvenir luggage tag, but you can also find pens, mugs, t-shirts, and my personal favorite, your very own inflatable Jiggly Kitten. In an act of pure genius, and blatant sexual harassment, an inflatable Jiggly Kitten had once shown up in Donna Spang's cubicle. But I digress.

I grabbed my bag and made my way to the car rental desk. A woman whose name tag told me her name was Gem, and that she was from Antigua, awaited me with a smile.

"Good afternoon ma'am," she said. "How may I help you?"

I handed Gem the reservation number that Margaret Sherman had given me before I left work on Friday. She hadn't wished me a nice trip or anything, just handed me a piece of paper and told me that if there was a problem she would be out of town. Gem typed away at her computer. All I had given her was a nine digit confirmation number, what on earth was she typing? I've typed entire reports and not hit as many keys. Finally the typing slowed to three second intervals, then five, then she stopped and pushed a form across the counter.

"Okay then, Miss Tessa Golden." She pointed her pen all around the form as she spoke. "You have a two door BMW compact convertible in red."

I choked a little bit. "BMW convertible?"

Flamhauser-Geist had never given me so much as a cupcake in appreciation of my four years of service. There had to be some mistake. I turned and looked at the line behind me to see if anybody else was hearing this.

"Yes, ma'am, that is what was reserved. I also have a message for you from a Ms. Kendra Stoltz. It says *Enjoy the Ride*. If you don't like red we do have another one available in blue."

"Um, no, red will be fine," I said, soaking in what I had just heard. Flamhauser-Geist had *requested* that I have a red BMW. What planet had I landed on? Maybe the plane had crashed. Was I dead? Maybe I should go check the news reports. I mean, sometimes people are dead and don't even realize it.

"You're a lucky girl, Miss Golden," said Gem. "Most companies send their employees off in un-cool sedans." She pushed a set of keys across the counter and pointed to the door where my car would be waiting. I thanked her more times than was necessary and giddily dragged my bags to the exit. The shock of the desert heat in my face was nothing compared to the shock of seeing a gorgeous, shiny, brand new, red, BMW convertible waiting for me at the curb. The porter helped me load my bags into the trunk, and then I slid behind the wheel.

I had arrived - and arrived in style.

5

As it turned out, my rental car came with a GPS, so the directions I had printed out and brought with me were not only unnecessary, but seriously lame. I threw them on the floor and drove out of the airport, obeying every command of the GPS who I immediately nicknamed Brad. Brad had a very soothing voice, as if he had been calibrated to instill calm and composure in the midst of the most horrid city traffic.

"You sly dog," I said to Brad, "directing me to your hotel."

It was immediate sensory overload as hotels, flashing lights, and beautiful people began popping up the closer I drove to The Strip. I stopped at a traffic light and turned up the radio - a mix of sunshine, endorphins, and lack of sleep coursing through my veins. I spent one of the happiest moments of my life at that traffic light, until I heard Brad struggling to tell me something. I reluctantly turned down the music.

"In point two miles, turn right onto Convention Center Drive."

"Shit!" I had been distracted by a billboard telling me how much food I could get for $4.95. You wouldn't believe it if I told you. I cut into the right lane, turned onto Convention Center Drive, and cruised into the driveway of my hotel. *Piece o' cake.*

I would love to tell you that Flamhauser-Geist had reserved me the penthouse suite with private swimming pool, or due to some crazy mix-up my room had been double booked and I would be bunking for three months with Zac Efron, but no such luck. I checked in at the front desk and was given the keys to a pretty standard suite. Though by "standard," I mean way nicer than my apartment back home. Pale yellow walls greeted me as I pushed open the door. Scented candles were scattered about and the furniture was straight out of Pottery Barn. I spotted a huge flat screen television through the French doors that separated the living area from the bedroom.

Not bad, I thought, dropping my bags to the floor. That was when I noticed the massive quantity of alcohol spread out on the sideboard. Bottles of Cruzan, Patron, Grey Goose, to name a few, all lined up around an assortment of martini, shot, and champagne glasses. A vase of yellow and peach roses was placed in the middle of it all. *Tessa,* said the card. I plucked it out and read the note.

Welcome! Just a little something to get you settled. See you Monday, Kendra.

Just a little something to get me settled? I looked from bottle to bottle and laughed at the thought of getting plastered all by myself on my very first night in Vegas. Who did she think I was going to drink all this with? I opened the refrigerator. It was devoid of food, but packed with beers. The clock on the microwave read 11:00 a.m. Well, if you take into account the time difference, it was technically 2:00 p.m. And if I was back home at a cook-out or a birthday party or something, I would probably be drinking a beer at 2:00 p.m.

Whatever.

I cracked one open. If I had to hang out by myself all weekend I might as well be good company. I flung myself onto the bed and stared around at my new home away from home. I was definitely not in the mood for unpacking. I was, however, in the mood for lounging by the hotel pool. I got back up and grabbed my carry-on bag. Inside was my toothbrush, a change of underwear, and the most wonderful green and white polka dot bikini ever created. If my luggage was lost, every single item in my suitcase could be easily replaced, including the t-shirt that I bought at Woodstock '94. That's what eBay's for, right? But this $300.00 bikini was the find of a lifetime, and so I kept it safely in my carry-on bag. I had found it on my very last day of shopping with Kara and it did the most amazing things for my body. I did not put it on my expense account, as Kara had suggested, but after seeing the car and the spread of alcohol I have a feeling Kendra may have approved it.

I got changed and stood in front of the full length mirror admiring myself for a few minutes. I swept my bangs to the side and added a little bit of bronzer to my cheeks. On second thought I pulled a giant pair of silver hoop earrings from my bag. I wasn't exactly swimming relay races here - most likely I wouldn't even leave the lounge chair.

"Damn, I look good," I said out loud to myself. "What a waste."

For a few seconds I entertained the idea of taking some cell phone pictures of myself and sending them to Nick.

"Don't be a psychopath," I said to my reflection. Then I

chugged the rest of my beer and headed for the pool.

***

Two hours and two frozen fruity cocktails later, I lay on my bed, showered and cozy in a hotel bathrobe, flipping through television channels. It had been *hot* out there and I was a bit redder than my mother would have liked. Jet lag, sun, and alcohol are an interesting mix. I was exhausted and burnt, but most definitely happy. I desperately needed a nap, but I had a cheeseburger and fries on their way up from room service and, at least for me, hunger tends to beat sleep. I surfed past home shopping channels, a cartoon moose wearing a detective hat, several games shows, and then -

"A Jarvis Brother's movie!" I had never been so delighted. There was a tiny man crawling around pretending that he was a baby. I laughed out loud at something I would not have found funny three hours earlier, settled back into the squishy down pillows, and fell asleep.

I spent the rest of my Saturday afternoon unpacking and venturing out to a grocery store so I could fill my fridge with something other than beer. I was in bed for the night by 9:30 p.m., and I suffered through quite a few strange dreams. In one of them I was playing poker with Tooth Model. I laid down my hand, a royal flush, and then he laid down his. Except instead of playing cards he was holding pictures of women he said he had slept with. One of the pictures was of rental desk Gem. "You slept with Gem?" I asked him. "We were in the army together," he replied. His pictures of women beat my royal flush and he took all my chips. Except they weren't chips. They were sets of false teeth, which made perfect sense.

I woke up bright and early on Sunday with the pleasant realization that I had not a single responsibility until Monday. I had nothing to clean because I had a maid, and I had nobody to visit because I didn't know a soul. I had an entire day to indulge in whatever the heck I felt like. The tourist information guide in my room informed me that The Forum Shops at Caesar's Palace had over 160 stores, and it became instantly clear that what I felt like doing was shopping.

I had the taxi let me off on The Strip rather than the hotel entrance so that I could have a little look around. The sidewalks were absolutely swarming with people. Everybody was carrying a beer or a three foot long frozen margarita, stopping to take pictures, and shouting to each other with excitement. I couldn't believe that this was actually a city where people lived and worked, and not an amusement park. I hadn't walked more than ten feet when I found myself being swept through a pack of men trying to shove what looked like playing cards in my face. By the time I emerged out the other side I had about ten cards in my hand and looked down to see what they were.

"Oh my God!" I laughed. Brooke, Julia, Claire, Melody, Summer, Candy, Ryanne, Christina, Danica, and Alexa. All prostitutes. All naked. They were also all available direct to my hotel room for as little as thirty-five dollars. I dumped the cards into the nearest trash can. These things literally covered the sidewalks. Everywhere I turned, lusty hookers stared up at me from the ground, their living counterparts ready and waiting for my phone call. I felt pretty sorry for them. I mean, they could probably get jobs at The Jiggly Kitty if they just applied. It wasn't the most respectable place on Earth, but at least the Jiggly Kittens don't have to have sex with anybody. Well, not with anybody they don't want to.

I kept walking until I finally found an entrance to Caesar's. I accidentally entered into the hotel lobby, which forced me to walk through miles of casino before being dumped out into the Forum Shops, where I stopped dead in my tracks. The Hallelujah chorus echoed in my ears as upscale store after upscale store stretched out before me. I looked up to see the coolest ceiling ever. It was painted to look like blue sky with clouds, and a nearby security guard, who noticed me staring up at it like a hick tourist, informed me that it changed color throughout the day. By nighttime it would be dark with stars. *That is exactly what we need at the office,* I thought.

A huge circular escalator brought me up and down between levels, and before I could even go into a single store, I was distracted by a show starting outside The Cheesecake Factory. Robotic characters rose up out of a fountain and acted out the story of the fall of Atlantis. As I stood there watching I couldn't help but think of Nick. This was the kind of place that you needed to share with somebody and I suddenly felt quite lonely, despite the hundreds of other shoppers around me. I wished that he was there with me so badly that I took my phone out of my purse to give him a call. I had one finger on his speed dial button when it started to ring.

Nick, read the Caller ID. A photo I had taken of him at the company's summer cook-out smiled back at me. Through some sort of cross-country mental telepathy he had sensed that I needed him. What further sign did I need that this was the man for me? Curse his happy marriage!

"Hello?" I answered.

"What's cookin' good lookin'?" asked my favorite voice in the world.

"I was just thinking about you!" I said, turning away from the show and taking a seat on a white marble bench.

"Freaky," he said. "I was just thinking about *you.* So how was the flight? How's Vegas? You're not already dating an Elvis impersonator are you? I know how you get when you have a few drinks."

"I totally am," I said. "The only problem is that he's a *fat* Elvis impersonator."

"Does that mean he's also an old Elvis impersonator?" asked Nick.

"Fat and old, you know how I like my men." I laughed.

"Don't go making me jealous now," said Nick. His voice softened a little and I was suddenly reminded of the kiss that he had blown me from his office window. Had he really just used the word *jealous*? This was certainly a new development. In all the years I'd known him, Nick had never once made any indication that he was jealous of me dating other guys. Even if we were talking about a fat, old, Elvis impersonator.

"You? Jealous?" I asked, playing along. "Give me a break."

"I'm serious," said Nick. "You're hot. You're going to have guys all over you out there. Just be careful, okay?"

Hot? Since when did Nick find me hot? My heart was suddenly pounding a mile a minute. Maybe I should have moved three thousand miles away a long time ago.

"Okay, *Dad*," I said. "I'll be just fine. You can't be jealous anyway, you're married remember?" *Remember when you ripped my heart out, fed it through the paper shredder, and then used it as confetti at your wedding reception?*

"Don't remind me," said Nick.

"Why? What's going on?"

"Nothing," he said. "Never mind. Meg and I are cool. Now tell me what you've really been up to."

I slumped down on the bench, slightly disappointed, and told him all about Tooth Model, the BMW, and everything else that had happened since my arrival. I told him that I was out shopping, and then, in a desperate attempt to steer the conversation back toward the romantic, I told him that I missed him.

"It's a little lonely out here right now," I said. "I just kind of wish that, um, that you were here too. Or, uh, you know, you or Kara."

"Yeah?" said Nick. "What would we, or you and Kara, be doing right now?"

"Well, there's a ton of alcohol in my room, so, you know, I think we could maybe figure something out."

Oh God, what was I saying? Maybe it was the distance that made me feel comfortable talking that way. Or maybe it was the fact that after so many years of nothing, Nick had finally opened a tiny window of interest and I couldn't resist seeing where it might lead. I think that on some level his being married only made my little game safer - knowing that no matter what I said, it could never become a reality. Well, probably never.

"I bet we could," said Nick. He cleared his throat. "You know, I'm really going to miss you tomorrow. Who am I supposed to complain to at work?"

"Donna Spang?" I suggested.

"I said complain *to*, not complain *about*."

"Right," I said. "Well, you still have Kara."

"She's not you."

My hands were sweating and shaking so badly that I thought I might actually drop my phone, or swoon like somebody in an old movie. *Do they sell smelling salts in this place?* I finally pulled myself together and was about to say something witty when Nick interrupted.

"Uh, hey Tess?" he said, almost in a whisper. "I gotta go. Megan's coming through the door."

"Oh, okay," I said, the smile falling from my face. I desperately did not want him to hang up. "I'll talk to you soon then. Say hi to Kara for me."

"Definitely," said Nick. "I, uh, um -" He seemed to be struggling to find some words. Unfortunately, they never came. "Bye, Tess."

"Bye, Nick."

I found myself alone again, even more painfully so than before he had called. And on top of that, I was now totally confused. Nick was jealous. Nick wasn't jealous. His marriage was messed up. His marriage was fine. Why did he need to hang up just because his wife came home? It's not like we were having phone sex. I mean, Megan knew we were friends.

"Enough of this," I said, getting up from the bench and heading in the direction of Juicy Couture. "It's time to shop!" An elderly woman glanced over at me like I was nuts, but I didn't care. Besides, who was the one wearing a windbreaker and a fanny pack in one of the ritziest shopping malls in Las

Vegas? Not me, old woman. Not me.

Yes, retail therapy was what I needed to get my mind off of my sorry excuse for a love life. There was no room for sad faces in a mall like this.

6

I stood looking up at the giant wall of reflective glass, tilting my head back as far as it could go to see to the very top of 1414 Howard Hughes Parkway. Palm trees lined the walkway leading into the home of Flamhauser-Geist's Las Vegas branch, which occupied three levels of this gorgeous architectural monstrosity. Nothing was visible through the windows. No desks, no photocopiers, no conference rooms full of stressed out engineers. All that could be seen from the outside of the building was the reflection of palm trees swaying peacefully in the breeze, as if the inside did not exist. I caught my own reflection in the first floor windows, staring up in awe like an uncouth hillbilly, but for the moment I didn't care. They don't often make buildings like this back home, and when they do they certainly don't reflect palm trees and sunshine. Working behind that glass, it seemed, could be nothing less than magnificent. I was lucky to be able to walk down this pathway each day, to pass by sand and cactus, and never catch a reflection of myself looking bedraggled and miserable from the rain or snow.

I smoothed out the new outfit that I'd bought during my

shopping trip on Sunday - sky blue blouse, black skirt, zebra print heels. One paycheck down, six to go. Hey, first impressions are important, right? And to my delight, my sunburn had developed into quite a nice little tan. I was looking good and feeling ready to take on the role of Administrative Assistant to not only the manager of this branch, but also the daughter of Mr. Sean Flamhauser. This was a man who had grown up in the slums of Boston, graduated in the top of his class at Northeastern University, and became co-founder of one of the most respected civil engineering firms in the country. I felt every bit the hot shot as I walked through the front doors and immediately tripped over the carpet.

"Ouch!" said the girl at the front desk, looking up from her computer. "Are you okay?"

"Awesome," I said, laughing at myself, and smoothing out my outfit for the second time. "Now that you think I'm a complete moron, can you please tell me where to find Flamhauser-Geist?"

She pointed to a bank of elevators. "They're on floors 30, 31, and 32. The manager, Ms. Stoltz, her office is on the 32nd. Once you're up there the receptionist, Roberta Mallard, will be able to help you." She looked me up and down, probably trying to figure out if I worked for The Jiggly Kitty. "Are you a client?"

"No, I'm actually Kendra, um, Ms. Stoltz's, new assistant. They shipped me out here from Massachusetts."

Her face changed slightly at the mention of the name Kendra, halfway between a sneer and something I couldn't quite identify.

"Oh, that's right. Marisa left to have her baby." She tucked a blonde curl behind her ear. "That girl was *huge*, you should have seen her. When I have kids I am not going to let myself get like that. No way. I mean she had literally turned into a whale."

"Literally into a whale?" I asked. "That must have been a sight." I wasn't quite sure how or why the conversation had turned to how fat Kendra's last assistant was, but I just smiled politely and let her continue.

"A total whale," she said. "So you're in for an interesting time. Let me give you a few pieces of advice straight off. If you ever need a ladies room with some privacy, use the fifth floor because those offices are unoccupied. Just don't let anybody see you because they'll know you had to go number two. Second, Roberta is a moron. If you need anything, don't go to her. Come to me. I don't work for your company, but I know more about it than she does. Third, there's a Fed Ex guy named Fitz, or Fartz, I don't really know which. But he does this thing where he pretends to drop a package so girls in the building will bend over to pick it up for him. Avoid him at all costs."

Boy could she talk. It was as if I was the first person to walk through those doors in ten years.

"I'll keep those things in mind," I said. "Thanks."

"I try to learn as much as I can about the people in this building. I talk to *everybody*. I would say I spend ninety percent of my day talking to people."

"Wow, really? Ninety percent?"

"Between eighty and ninety. There's not much else to do

down here. Oh, one last thing. Ms. Stoltz's husband is some kind of power hungry pervert. He works here too, and he always comes down to ask me to do things for him."

The phone on the reception desk had been ringing for the last twenty seconds, but she ignored it.

"Like I said, I don't even work for your company, but he doesn't care. I think he actually feels like he can get away with sexual harassment because of that. I mean one time," she leaned in closer to me, "he insisted on helping me move some boxes that I totally didn't need any help with. When he asked me where I wanted them I said 'anywhere,' and he goes 'good because I'll put it anywhere you want it."

"Gross!" I said, crinkling my nose. But that sounded about right. The same guy who had asked me to play Twister at the Christmas party had quite the reputation around the office as well.

"Exactly. So beware. Marisa used to avoid him like the plague." She rolled over to grab something off the printer. "My name's Charlene, by the way."

"Tessa." I smiled and shook her hand. The hand shake caused Charlene to stop talking for about three seconds, and I jumped at the opportunity to excuse myself. I thanked her again for all her helpful, though somewhat disturbing, information, and watched myself walk toward the shiny golden elevators doors. Everything in this building was highly reflective. I came out on the 32nd floor across from a set of heavy glass doors outlined in cherry trim. Gold lettering above the door frame read *Flamhauser-Geist* and I had the weird sensation of being in an alternate universe.

I pulled open the door and immediately recognized Kendra

standing by the reception desk, apparently awaiting my arrival. She looked different from the last time I'd seen her, without her gown and her diamonds, but she was still one of the most beautiful people I have ever met. Her long blonde hair fell in waves that my own hair could only dream about. Where her clingy black sweater dress ended, knee high leather boots took over. Miles of gold chains coiled themselves around her neck. Her makeup looked professionally done, though I knew that was impossible on a Monday morning. She was simply Engineering Barbie in the flesh. The older woman seated at the desk next to her, who I took to be the useless Roberta Mallard, looked annoyed.

"Tessa!" Kendra greeted me with such familiarity and enthusiasm that I almost turned to check if her long lost friend Tessa had walked in behind me.

"Kendra!" I held out my hand for a shake, but she instead pulled me in for a hug. She even smelled expensive.

"Thank you *so* much for coming! How's the car? And the hotel? Did you find the office okay?" It was hard to keep track of all the questions. It seemed that everybody in the building talked a mile a minute.

"Yes, thank you!" I said. "Everything is unbelievable. You really shouldn't have given me all those things. I'm totally spoiled."

"Oh please! It was a huge deal for you to pack up and come out here like this. It's the *least* I could do." She turned to Roberta, who was looking more annoyed by the minute. "Roberta, I'd like you to meet my new assistant, Tessa. Tessa, this is Roberta, our receptionist."

"Nice to meet you," said Roberta, giving me the once-over.

I wonder if women honestly think you don't notice when they do that. She stared at my boobs for at least five seconds before moving down to check out the size of my waist. Donna Spang may have met her match.

"You too," I said, giving her the once-over right back. She looked to be in her mid-forties, and thin as a rail, which is not always a good look for somebody her age. Boobs? No where to be found.

"Aren't you a tiny little thing," she said. "Do you eat?"

"Excuse me?"

"You're so thin. I myself never have much of an appetite." She motioned to an uneaten apple on her desk.

"I eat a lot, actually," I said. I gave Kendra a confused look.

"I don't think Tessa wants to discuss this right now, Roberta," said Kendra, rolling her eyes. "Come on, I'll show you to your desk."

"What's with her?" I asked as we headed across the office. We passed cubicle after cubicle but showed no signs of slowing down.

"Oh, she's just weight obsessed," said Kendra. "The woman prides herself on eating nothing but raisins and lettuce. We all figure she goes home every night and gorges on Doritos. You should have heard her talk about Marisa after she gained all that pregnancy weight. Pure disgust."

"You know that's the second time in about fifteen minutes that somebody has mentioned Marisa's weight?" I smiled back at a couple of cute guys who were talking next to a water cooler .

"That's because we have more than a few busybodies in this building. But you'll grow to love them."

"Yeah, we had busybodies back in Massachusetts too," I said. "But the love thing never really happened."

We finally arrived at the opposite end of the building where a plaque that read "Kendra Stoltz" was fastened to the door of the corner office. On the door of the office directly next to it was a plaque taped over with a piece of paper that read "Tessa Golden." Yes, that's right, an *office*. My office.

"Home sweet home," said Kendra, stepping in ahead of me. An expanse of windows lined the wall in front of us, and I gasped at the view of the city that I had from the 32nd story. How on earth would I ever be able to work? I peeled myself away from the windows long enough to soak in the rest of my surroundings. Everything was either white, black, or lilac, and everything was new. I could not see so much as an outdated paperclip. The flat panel monitor on the desk was one of the most impressive features, as back home my monitor is about three feet deep and I am physically incapable of lifting it. This was turning out to be an alternate universe indeed. Lilac shag carpeting covered the floor beneath a huge white leather desk chair. I sat down and spun around a couple of times. A fish tank stood to the right of the door, filled with exotic looking fish and lilac colored gravel.

"Holy shit," I said. I looked up at Kendra and shook my head. "Do you have any idea what my other office is like? Wait, let me rephrase that. Do you have any idea what my *cubicle* was like?"

"That's the beauty of working for me. I treat my employees the way I would want to be treated." She picked a remote control up off the bookshelves and pushed a button. Classical music began playing from speakers positioned around the room. "And I wouldn't expect anything less than the best." She watched for my reaction and snorted when I mouthed the words "holy shit" again. I couldn't seem to think of anything else to say.

"I guess Marisa was into classical," she said. "But you can play whatever you like. I have a ton of CD's if you want to borrow anything."

"Yes, definitely. Thank you!" I said. "Really, Kendra, I'm at a loss for words here. I can't even believe we work the way we do back in Massachusetts. It's like a prison camp compared to this."

"Well, when you're two degrees from the owner of the company, you reap the benefits." She shrugged and pulled open the door of a mini refrigerator to reveal a case of beer and several bottles of wine. "For after hours."

"Nice," I said. "But I think I need to let all of this sink in before I'll be ready for any after hours festivities."

"Fair enough," said Kendra. "I'll let you get settled. Your email is all set up, and you have full internet access. I know the fuddy-duddies in HR block certain websites, but that doesn't apply here." She gave me a wink. "Other than being way less crappy, we're very similar to your old office in terms of the work we do. It should be smooth sailing for you."

Kendra left me alone and headed back into her own office where she must have picked up another remote control, because I heard the muffled sounds of Eminem filtering through the wall.

I smiled to myself as I scrolled through my email, finding it hard not to spin around and stare out the windows. There weren't many emails to scroll through anyway, just a few office-wide ones from people I did not yet know, informing me that they were heading out on site visits to cities that I had never heard of. Everything about my life was new and fresh, down to the very clothes that I was wearing.

Ah, screw it.

I abandoned my email and rolled over to the window. This was the change that I needed, I could feel it in my bones. My tired, uninspired bones were slowly but surely coming back to life. Maybe I would start working on my art again while I was out here. Not just paperclip and pushpin art, but the kind of stuff that I did back in college. I mean, sure I was in Las Vegas and there were plenty of things to distract me on the weekends, but in all honesty, who was I going to hang out with? I was probably going to be spending a lot of time alone in my hotel room, and if I ever wanted to dig myself out of this secretarial hole, now would be the perfect time to get started.

7

A knock at the door startled me from my thoughts. I turned around to find a pretty woman, who I guessed to be in her fifties, wearing a peach blouse, white pants, and a smoking hot pair of gold stilettos. She smiled and introduced herself as Sharon Bloom, head of Human Resources. Margaret Sherman she was not. When Margaret Sherman's sour face walks into a room you want to jump out the window, but Sharon practically lit the place up. She spent the next hour showing me around the office and introducing me to about three thousand people whose names I immediately forgot. We zigzagged our way through all three floors, meeting engineers, draftsmen, secretaries, accountants, human resources reps, and countless other people, who, in all honesty, I would probably never see again for the duration of my three months in Vegas.

"Oh," said Sharon after we had arrived back outside my office, "I almost forgot to introduce you to Chris and Dan. You'll be working quite a bit with those two, come on."

I followed Sharon into the office immediately next to mine and suddenly felt like I was back in college. Their office was at least twice the size of my own but resembled a dorm room more than a workspace. It was divided down the middle by two video game chairs positioned in front of a flat screen television. A trophy on top of the mini-fridge read *Flamhauser-Geist Ping-Pong Champions - 2008,* and a row of empty beer cans lined the windowsill behind the television. Seated in the game chairs were the two cute guys I had smiled at by the water cooler.

"Tessa, this is Chris Brewer and Dan Bryant," said Sharon. "Dan is the one annihilating aliens at the moment."

"Nice to meet you," said Chris. He jumped up to shake my hand. "We were just taking a little, uh, break." He glanced at his watch, seeming to remember that it wasn't anywhere close to lunch time. "Kendra got us the video games as sort of a stress reliever."

"Oh, please," I said. "No need to explain to me!" I smiled when I noticed a familiar emblem on the front of his polo shirt - a pink kitten caught mid-spin around a stripper pole. "Classy shirt, by the way."

"Yeah? I've got about six more at home," said Chris. "Dan and I work on The Jiggly Kitty account with Kendra, so we're always getting free goodies."

"So what's the Kitty like back in Massachusetts?" asked Dan over his shoulder.

"It's okay, I guess. Relatively speaking." I shrugged. "I've only been to one of them, and just one time. I don't really have much to compare it to."

"Really?" said Dan. "Chris and I go there for lunch everyday. We design the parking lot, and they give us free access to the buffet. It's a sweet little deal we have worked out."

"He's joking," said Chris, turning slightly pink. "I wouldn't eat lunch at a strip club if my life depended on it."

"But dinner you're cool with?" I asked.

"And what kind of situation would lead to your life depending on eating lunch at a strip club?" asked Dan.

"Okay, okay," interrupted Sharon. "You've officially met Chris and Dan, shall we move on? She rolled her eyes and gently pulled me by the elbow as a signal that it was time to move on to meet much less interesting people.

"You know," I said, as we turned to leave, "it's much colder in Massachusetts. So I think the strippers just wear more clothes."

***

As soon as I had settled back into my office, Chris appeared with a legal pad full of handwritten scribbles that needed to be typed.

"I hate to do this to you on your first day," he said.

"Whatever," I told him, "I'm a secretary, typing is my sole purpose in life."

"Cool, thanks." He dropped the papers in front of me, along with a snack sized Butterfinger bar. "And also, that's a little sad."

I laughed. "Well, someday I hope to find another purpose. Perhaps photocopying."

"It's good to have goals," he said. He lingered in my doorway a bit and then motioned to the candy. "Dan and I have stock in Nestle, so um, come by whenever you want." His cheeks turned pink for the second time since I'd met him, and he adjusted his glasses. He smiled sheepishly at me and then quickly disappeared from my doorway.

Chris was kind of hot in a Clark Kent sort of way, and he was already nicer than ninety percent of the people I worked with back home. A quick scan of his hand had revealed no wedding ring.

"Get a grip, Tessa. You have a perfectly nice married man waiting for you back home." I shook the thought from my head and dove into my first assignment.

***

I had a meeting with Kendra before lunch, as she wanted to give me the rundown on Jiggly Kitty President, and Flamhauser-Geist VIP client, Rob Dorfman, before he came in for his weekly status meeting the next day. The term "VIP client" refers to someone whose butt must be kissed on a regular basis, regardless of how much you despise their personality, and Rob Dorfman's personality ranked right up there with dog shit and rocks. You would think that somebody whose entire life and business was focused around beautiful naked women would have something to smile about, but this was not the case. I think that when Rob Dorfman looks at a stripper all he sees is dollar signs, and they tend to get in the way of the important parts. He is not a pleasant man to say the least, and back in Massachusetts I was lucky enough to only deal with him over the telephone. But since The Jiggly Kitty is headquartered here in Las Vegas, my luck was about to run out.

While Kendra rifled through one of her desk drawers I

wandered around her office looking at the paintings on the walls. They were quite good. An old man and a little boy, three girls on a bench. They were mostly of people doing everyday things, and I couldn't help but notice that the colors of each painting accented the office decor perfectly, as if they had been painted to match. I was surprised to see the initials KS painted lightly in the corner, and was about to ask Kendra if she had painted them herself, when her desk drawer slammed shut.

"This," she said, holding up an 8 x10 photograph, "is Rob Dorfman."

She actually had a picture of the guy in her desk. Four smiling people were giving a thumbs up in front of a glass door sporting The Jiggly Kitty logo. The photo had been taken at the grand opening of the latest Jiggly Kitty project, and from the smiles on their faces you would think they had found a cure for cancer. The two men on the outside I did not recognize, but there was Kendra in the middle, and next to her, she pointed out, was Rob Dorfman. I busted out laughing. He was rosy cheeked and about four inches shorter than her. His suit probably cost more than I make in a year, but he was practically swimming in it.

Son of a bitch, I thought, *he looks like a kid at his Bar Mitzvah.*

"No way!" I said looking up at Kendra. "How the heck old is he?" All the years that I had spent bowing down to the little slime ball, calling him "Sir," and *this* is what he looked like? I suddenly didn't feel like laughing anymore.

"Twenty-six," she said. "Didn't you know?"

"No!" I said. "I always assumed he was in his forties!"

"Nope. He started the Kitty right out of college. His dad

gave him a handful of millions to start up his own business, and that's what he came up with. The little freak."

I handed Kendra back the photograph and fell into her white leather couch. I could not believe that I had actually called somebody two years younger than me "Sir."

"You should hear the way he speaks to *me*," she said. "But Dad tells me that his wish is my command, so what choice do I have?" She plopped down on the couch next to me and continued to explain that we had six projects in the works for Jiggly Kitty's throughout Nevada and Arizona, and that every Tuesday morning Rob came by the office to check on their progress.

Arrangements had to be made each week before his big arrival. First off, Rob refused to drink Flamhauser-Geist brewed coffee, yet he also refused to bring his own, so it was my responsibility to fetch him a Venti low-fat, no whip, mocha from Starbucks. Even worse, I must time the coffee purchase perfectly, because if it was not piping hot I would be in for a verbal assault. Second, the two potted palm trees in the conference room must be relocated due to a severe allergic reaction he had in Hawaii when he was four. Finally, all pages over the office intercom must cease because Rob cannot stand the sound of Roberta Mallard's voice. I will admit that the last rule made me giggle. Kendra went through about fifteen other rules and requirements, when I put my hand up and stopped her.

"What about the men's room?" I asked. "Don't tell me that he uses the same facilities as the rest of us plebeians?"

"Believe it or not, he actually does poop with the commoners." She cleared her throat and looked down at her lap. "But there is one tiny detail."

"What's that?"

"It's your job to wipe."

8

Okay, okay, so it wasn't *really* my job to wipe, but everything else Kendra had told me was true. It was 10:25 a.m. on Tuesday, and I nervously checked the clock on my computer for the millionth time. The two potted palm trees had been dragged into the storage room, Roberta had been told to keep her mouth shut, and in five minutes I would be leaving for Starbucks. God willing, I would be back a few minutes before Rob's arrival toting a Venti low-fat no whip mocha. If there is one thing I have learned from being an administrative assistant, it is that *you are always to blame.* Let's say that for some odd reason Starbucks is unable to make mochas today. I would fully expect Rob to berate me in front of my coworkers for being such a stupid idiot that I didn't have the foresight to go to a Starbucks that had mocha-making capabilities. Keeping that in mind, I mapped out the locations of two other local Starbucks just in case anything went wrong.

This is my fucking life, I thought as I closed out of Google Maps.

While blaming the assistant comes naturally for a person like Rob Dorfman - all managers, clients, and other assorted higher-ups are guilty of it as well. Take Fed Ex for example. Once a package of precious engineering plans has been properly labeled and deposited into a drop box, one would think that full responsibility is then transferred to Federal Express. That is not quite true. The assistant's responsibility does not end until that package arrives safely on the desk of whom it was intended.

If the Fed Ex truck breaks down, or the plane crashes, or the delivery man drops dead, those things are all your fault. Of course they won't say it explicitly. Your boss could never look you in the eye and say "Tessa, it is your fault that Joe Delivery man ate one too many blocks of cheese and had a heart attack en route to town hall," because to say it is to sound ridiculous. But the thought is in their head, even if it is on a subconscious level. They need to blame somebody, and Federal Express is much too general of a concept when you, an idiot human being, are conveniently standing right there in front of them.

Luckily, Starbucks was in perfect working order and I was back at the office five minutes before Rob's red carpet arrival. I said hello to Charlene and stepped into the elevator. Just as the doors were about to close a rosy cheeked tyke of a man came rushing through the front entrance and shouted at me to hold the elevator.

The lack of a "please" or "thank you," plus the fact that I had just seen his picture, confirmed that I was about to share an elevator with the dreaded Rob Dorfman himself.

"Thirty-two," he commanded, stepping in beside me. He couldn't even push his own floor button.

"Thirty-two," I repeated. "Me too."

I smiled at him as I pushed the button, but he couldn't have possibly shown any less of an interest in me. The floor numbers lit up one by one as we rode in silence. I restrained myself from taking a sip of his coffee and letting out one of those sounds you make after drinking a Coca-Cola on a ninety degree day. He exited the elevator ahead of me, not bothering to hold the office door open, and scurried straight to reception where I heard him exchange a few heated words with Roberta. I wonder if she had the nerve to ask Rob Dorfman about his eating habits.

I headed back to my office where I found Kendra dropping off a stack of documents for photocopying.

"He's here," I said, trading her the coffee for the documents.

"God help us. Wish me luck!" She thanked me for the coffee then made the sign of the cross over her chest. "And bring these into the conference room when you're done, please."

As she took off for the conference room, I heard voices coming from Chris and Dan's office. I stopped in on my way to the photocopier to see what they were up to.

"You're smart, you're funny, and people like you!" said Dan. He pointed a red pen in Chris's direction from behind his desk.

"So are you, buddy," said Chris, pointing a blue pen right back. "And don't let anybody tell you differently."

"You know this is ridiculous," I said. "He's just a man. A tiny, childlike, little man. Nobody should cause this kind of fear in other people. Unless you're a murderer or something."

"Tessa, I wouldn't be surprised if he was," said Chris.

"Didn't you know?" asked Dan. "Chris and I are the fifth set of engineers to use this office."

"Once you miss a deadline, that's it." Chris's face was dead serious. "Engineer corpses have been turning up all over Vegas."

"That's too bad," I laughed. "I was just starting to like you guys."

"It's a high risk profession we've chosen," said Dan.

They gathered up their notepads and plans and solemnly shuffled toward the conference room.

"Good luck," I called after them.

The documents that I needed to copy were in regard to a Jiggly Kitty project in the City of Riverlin, Nevada. That was the main subject of today's meeting as our filing deadline with the Zoning Commission was coming up quickly. The only section of Riverlin that allows adult entertainment establishments is the Industrial Zone. And even in the Industrial Zone - a place that is also home to flea markets, tattoo parlors, and meat packing plants - a strip club is only allowed after obtaining a Special Permit. Kendra and Chris had presented their request for a Special Permit before the Zoning Commission back in December, and the hearing was a complete disaster.

The Commission is made up of seven members, five of whom you don't need to hear about. The sixth member is an established pervert and Jiggly Kitty supporter named Jasper Quick, and the seventh is a sweet but clueless older woman named Beatrice Miller. Beatrice Miller had been genuinely impressed by how well Kendra and Chris had put together their presentation, and she spoke to them as if they were two schoolchildren presenting at the science fair. The fact that they were discussing construction of a strip club in the city where her grandchildren lived did not seem to phase her. She simply remarked that Kendra reminded her of her daughter, and that the Jiggly Kitty logo was adorable. Dan was pretty sure she thought The Jiggly Kitty had something to do with cats.

The rest of the Zoning Commission, aside from Jasper Quick who, according to Chris, didn't take his eyes off of Kendra's ass for the entirety of the hearing, ripped the presentation to shreds. They nit-picked every aspect of the parking lot, the signs, the landscaping, you name it. The neon pink kitten spinning around a stripper pole that Beatrice found adorable, the rest of the Commission called obnoxious and blaring. They felt that traffic exiting the parking lot would interfere with traffic on the main road and requested that we install a traffic light. It seemed that for a city that wasn't too keen on strip joints, they certainly were planning for a lot of customers. The hearing was continued for one month, and they told Kendra and Chris to come back when they had designed an establishment that "more harmoniously fit into the spirit of Riverlin" They actually said that. The Jiggly Kitty, banished to a part of town that contains slaughterhouses, now must have the outward appearance of an 18th century bed and breakfast. The irony is spectacular.

I laid my stack of documents in the feed tray on top of the photocopier and said a silent prayer. I have never worked anywhere that had a properly functioning photocopier. Particularly the machine in our Massachusetts office - that thing malfunctioned on a daily basis. And of course, as an admin, I was expected to know not only how to clear all paper jams, but also the interpretation of every error code that appeared onscreen including such classics as MALFUNCTION 3DFQR4, ERROR CODE 6Q#8! and ALERT %729&1.

The reason I was so nervous was because what Kendra had given me were original legal documents borrowed from Rob Dorfman. Handing him back a stack of crinkled, torn, most likely irreplaceable, pages was not on my to-do list, so I held my breath as page after page was successfully drawn into the copier and shot out the other side. The job was about seventy-five percent complete when the ear-splitting squeal of a car accident and a crinkle of paper that will haunt me until the day I die caused the copier to come to a screeching halt.

Shit!

A flashing diagram showed paper jams in every possible place that there could be paper jams. I opened and shut trap doors and compartments, pulling out sheet after sheet of crumpled paper, relieved every time I didn't see the bright blue ink of an original stamp or signature.

Then I opened the side panel.

Deep within the bowels, wound tightly around a roller, was blue ink.

Son of a bitch, you piece of garbage, you piece of shitty garbage -

I ignored all warnings printed on the machine and plunged my hand inside. A large red circle with a slash through several bolts of lightning? No matter. It was do or die time and I couldn't be worried about minor details such as electricity or my personal safety. Do you think Rob Dorfman would care if I fried my arm off? No, all he cared about was getting his documents back in one piece. I had *two* arms after all, but he only had *one* set of documents. It was a matter of simple math.

I could just barely reach the roller with the tip of my index finger. It was extremely hot and difficult to turn, but slowly it was moving. Just when my finger felt as if it was going to snap, the paper came loose.

"Yes!" I yelled, holding the page up over my head like some kind of secretarial trophy. The damage was not too bad. I smoothed it out as best I could, and hid it in the middle of the stack. Rob wouldn't notice until he was back in his own office, and by that point, who cared? I finished up the rest of the copies without any trouble and headed for the conference room where I hoped to just slip in, drop them off, and slip back out.

Kendra was seated at the head of the long conference table. Chris and Dan sat next to each other with their back to the door, leaving Rob sitting directly across from them, facing me, as I walked in. I smile at him, wondering if he even recognized me as the girl from the elevator. But his little boy face only glared back with icy blue dagger eyes, as if I had just punched a seal cub in the face. The tension was so thick that I was actually glad, at that moment, that my responsibilities only went as far as making photo copies. I nearly had a heart attack when that page got crumpled, I couldn't even imagine what Kendra, Chris, and Dan felt like when something that Rob had spent thousands of dollars on didn't go right.

"I'll take those, Tessa. Thank you," said Kendra. She held out a hand to me while the other one continued sketching red lines onto the set of plans in front of her. I gave them to her and had one foot out the door when I heard my name again.

"Tessa," she said. "Do you mind staying for the rest of the

meeting? We could really use somebody to take notes."

No!

"Sure," I said. I grabbed a yellow legal pad and took a seat at the opposite end of the table. I had never been asked to take notes at a meeting before, and if this had been a meeting between normal people I may have asked Kendra exactly what type of things she needed written down. But since my sheer presence in the room was already grating on Rob's nerves, I decided to keep my mouth shut.

"Where were we?" asked Rob. "We're wasting time here."

"Well," said Kendra, "I was just explaining that if we reduced the size of the building, we could also reduce the amount of parking and increase the landscaping. These are the kinds of things that the Zoning Commission would like to see."

"I don't think so," said Rob. Kendra glanced up at Chris and Dan, who in turn exchanged confused looks.

"What do you mean?" asked Kendra.

"I mean, The Jiggly Kitty doesn't change for anybody. Each one is built to my specifications regardless of what city it's in. Am I not paying you to do what I ask?"

"Right," said Kendra. "But if we squeeze a full sized building onto this tiny plot of land, we're asking the city to make a lot of exceptions to their zoning code. Do you really think they're going to go along with that? Especially after they told us to come back with a design that 'fit more harmoniously into the spirit of Riverlin'?"

"Shh!" said Rob, holding his finger up in front of Kendra's face. He turned to Chris and Dan. "What would *you* two geniuses suggest?" He leaned back in his chair and pressed his fingertips together.

I started sketching a little bit in my notebook to appear busy as I didn't want him to turn his wrath on me.

"Well," said Chris, sitting up straighter in his chair and rubbing the back of his neck. "For starters, the VIP room to the rear would need to lose the trampoline section. It extends the building too close to the wetlands out back."

"And if we have to go before the Conservation Commission, they will never approve us," added Kendra. "They hate us too."

"Also," said Dan, "the idea about reserved parking spaces for curbside lap dances will need to be eliminated. We're low on parking even without those."

"Those spaces will make me a fortune," said Rob.

"The Zoning Commission doesn't care if you make money," said Kendra.

"Plus, I believe there are laws against outdoor nudity," said Chris.

"Look," said Rob. "All of these problems don't mean shit to me. I have always been able to get *my* clubs built to *my* specifications. You idiots act like we've never worked together before."

"We're just trying to compromise," said Kendra. "We need to be willing to make some adjustments if we want any chance of getting approved."

"I have never made adjustments. Adjustments are made for me. For as long as you've known me have I ever abided by a rule that I didn't like?"

"No," said Kendra. "You have not."
"And have I ever had a problem getting my approvals?"

"No," said Kendra, staring down at the table. "You always manage to pull it off. But what you don't seem to understand is that I need to at least *try* to practice some ethics."

Boy was it getting juicy. I kept my head down, buried in my notebook.

"You people do what I pay you to do, and I'll worry about *ethics*," said Rob.

"And by ethics you mean, what?" asked Chris. "Bribery?"

An involuntary gasp escaped me and I tried to cover it by clearing my throat. Rob shot me my second dirty look of the day. But I couldn't help it. I was very impressed by Chris's nerve to stand up to him. To be honest, I was very impressed with all three of their abilities to make as much of an argument as they did. It was all in vain, of course, but truly a valiant effort.

"Excuse me?" hissed Rob.

"What?" Chris shrugged. "I shouldn't have said it? You made it pretty obvious that that's what we're talking about."

"Chris!" said Kendra. "Stop it. Rob, I'm sorry, he's a little out of sorts today."

"Out of sorts?" said Chris. "What am I, six?"

"This meeting's over," snapped Rob. He stood up, grabbed his briefcase, and looked down at the four of us. His rosy cheeks were giving off quite a glow. I could definitely picture him playing video games in his pajamas.

"You just do what I say and keep your noses out of the rest of my business. And learn a little *respect* while you're at it." He pointed at Chris. "Or you'll find yourself at the back of the unemployment line." He focused his daggers back on Kendra. "Don't forget that there is nothing stopping me from taking my business to Richardson-Fleiss."

Richardson-Fleiss was one of our competitors. They worked for less money than us.

"Understood," said Kendra. She flashed a crazed smile at us as she stood up to walk Rob out of the conference room.

"Wait," said Rob, holding his hand up in her face for the second time. I shrank down a little bit in my chair because he had started shuffling through the stack of documents I had given back to him. "What the hell is this?" He pulled the crumpled blue signature sheet from the stack.

"There was, um, a little trouble with the copier," I squeaked.

"The *simplest* task," he said to me. "Son of a -"

"Alright then!" interrupted Kendra. She put her hand on Rob's shoulder and gently directed him out of the conference room. I expected him to fling her hand away, but for some creepy reason he allowed it. I didn't breathe again until they had left the room. Chris, Dan, and I sat looking at each other in silence for a few seconds.

"I thought that went well," said Dan.

"I can't believe you talked to him like that!" I looked at Chris in awe and chewed on the cap of my pen.

"I'm almost at my breaking point with that guy." He leaned his head back in the leather chair and pushed his glasses up, rubbing his eyes. "And by 'almost' I mean I reached it about three years ago."

"Maybe this will help." I slid my yellow legal pad across the table. On it was a hasty sketch of Rob Dorfman spinning around a stripper pole in a three piece suit.

Dan snorted. "Well aren't you a good little note taker!"

"Nice work," said Chris. "You can't handle the simplest tasks, but you sure can draw."

"It's amazing what the feeble secretarial mind is capable of," I said.

As we left the conference room I was struck by that feeling of relief that you get after leaving the dentist's office. You know, the one where you realize that you don't have to go back for another six months. I had one whole week before Rob's next visit, and I would savor every second.

9

On the following Tuesday Kendra didn't show up for work. Nobody in the office had heard from her all morning, and by ten o'clock Chris and Dan had entered into panic mode. Nothing short of death was excusable for missing the weekly Dorfman meeting, even if you were the boss's daughter. And without Kendra, Chris and Dan would have to face the meeting, and a furious Rob Dorfman, all by themselves. He would take her not being there as a personal insult and proof of our incompetence. Richardson-Fleiss would soon have a new client on their hands.

I stood in the window of Chris and Dan's office, looking out over the city.

"What if something happened to her?" I wondered aloud. "Has she ever done this before?"

"No," said Dan. " She's flakey but she's always the first one here. And she would never be late on a Dorfman day." His left leg bounced up and down like mad.

Chris was hunched over his drafting table, red pen in hand, frantically marking up a set of Jiggly Kitty plans. "You'd better try calling her house," he said over his shoulder.

"I already tried that," I sighed. "Nobody answered."

I left their office and reluctantly walked over to the reception desk. If Kendra had called in, Roberta would be the first to know. I found her reading a copy of *Woman's Day*, opened to a recipe for rack of lamb.

"Are you making that tonight?" I asked.

She looked up at me like I had just suggested she come to work naked next Thursday.

"Oh goodness, no," she said. "I just like to look at the pictures. If I so much as smelled a meal like that I would gain twelve pounds." She turned the page with her bony wrist.

"You know, Roberta," I said, "you're very skinny. You really don't need to worry about your weight so much."

She shot me that look again - like I had suggested she come to work naked wearing cowboy boots.

"You sound just like my doctor," she said. "Poor thing is at least twenty pounds overweight."

My brain screamed at me to end the conversation, so I changed the subject and asked if she had heard anything from Kendra. She had not. I wished her luck with her rack of lamb and decided to go see Charlene in the lobby.

"But I'm not making it!" Roberta shouted after me.

I found Charlene watering plants by the front windows.

"Hey!" she said. "You just missed Fartz! He looked pretty hammered this morning, like he's been out all night - hey, what's wrong? You look like a wreck."

I thanked her for the compliment and then explained the predicament I was in.

"The little squirt's going to murder us if Kendra's not here." I pinched the leaves of a fern tightly between my fingers.

"Why don't you swing by her house?" she suggested, gently prying my fingers off the plant. "I have home addresses for everybody in the building in my computer. Makes you feel safe, huh?" She rolled her eyes and put the watering can back under her desk. She wrote the address down on a purple post-it note.

I thanked her for the help, and pushed my way through the heavy glass doors, onward with my mission.

***

Over the past few days I had grown to expect glamour and excess around every corner, so I was probably not as shocked as I should have been when I pulled into the driveway of 6 Whispering Palm Drive. I parked behind a blue BMW, which I assumed to be Kendra's, and surveyed the outside of the house for signs of burglary. I didn't really want to walk in on something I would regret. Everything seemed normal. Well, everything except the sheer enormity and gorgeousness of the place.

How do I even begin to describe it? The house was made up of mostly windows. Five arch shaped windows lined the front wall of the second level, and below them was the front door, nestled between two sets of massive bay windows. To the left, the house jutted out into a circular room topped off by a turret. The house had a turret for Christ sake. The turret alone was larger than my entire apartment back home. A rolling green lawn, landscaped to perfection and dotted with palm trees, topped everything off like a cherry on a very expensive cake.

The street was eerily quiet as most people had already gone to work. The only sign of life came from a man pulling weeds across the street.

"Excuse me," I shouted. "Have you seen anybody come out of this house today?"

The man stopped what he was doing and wiped the sweat from his forehead with the back of his gardening glove.

"Just Mr. Stoltz," he shouted back. " He left about eight o'clock with a suitcase. Haven't seen his wife today though. Everything okay?"

"I'm not sure. Thanks!" I walked up the front steps and rang the doorbell.

Nothing.

The last thing I needed to start my second week of work was to find my boss murdered by her psychotic husband, as I'd seen happen in plenty of *Lifetime* movies. Some of those are based on true stories, you know. Or maybe she had fallen down the stairs and was laying in a grotesque heap on the floor. Maybe she had committed suicide in the bathtub and what I was about to see would traumatize me for life! Maybe I should just get back on a plane and go home to Massachusetts, just pretend I was never here, just -

Oh don't be such an idiot.

"Kendra? Kendraaa?" I gave up the doorbell and started knocking on the door pretty loudly.

Still nothing. Then, in a stroke of genius, I tried the knob. It turned, and the door opened. An unlocked door was not necessarily the best sign, but at least I was in. I immediately checked the bottom of the staircase for a mangled body, but there was nobody there. So far so good. Now to check all the bathtubs.

"Kendra?" I made my way slowly into the house and walked around the living room to the right of the stairs. Despite the dread I felt I couldn't help but notice how gorgeous the place was from the inside as well. Hanging over the fireplace was a painting of the same style I had seen in Kendra's office. The colors matched the room as if the room had been planned around it, or vice-versa. The initials KS once again graced the corner. Several framed pictures lined the mantel, but several others lay broken on the floor. I turned one of the frames over and saw the faces of Kendra and the scum bag I recognized from the Christmas party as her husband Todd, smiling at me from the rim of the Grand Canyon.

I put the frame back on the mantel and headed up the stairs. I stepped carefully around a trail of men's shirts, belts, watches, and other personal items that appeared to have been dumped off the second floor balcony.

Burglars?

My heart racing, I ran back downstairs and grabbed a poker from the fireplace. I held it poised over my right shoulder as I returned to the second floor and began peeking into room after room. I was fully prepared to club the son of a bitch who had murdered my boss, when I stumbled upon the master bedroom. There in bed, staring at the ceiling, but undoubtedly alive, was Kendra. She lay on top of the blankets wrapped in a huge pink bathrobe - her face was splotchy from crying and her hair was spread out in a tangled halo on the pillow. A snowstorm of pink tissues littered the bed and the surrounding floor.

"Hey," I said, knocking gently on the open door and lowering my weapon. "There you are. We've been worried sick." I took the approach of sounding like my mother, or like I was talking to an elderly person, as I wasn't exactly sure what else to say. Kendra didn't even look at me or seem surprised that I was there in her house. She just kept staring up at the ceiling. I looked up there too, in case I was missing something, but it was just a ceiling.

"He's gone," she said to the plaster swirls.

"Who?" I asked like an idiot. Of course I knew *who*, but what else could I say?

"Todd. My *husband*." She emphasized the word husband not in a "you should know who Todd is" way, but rather in a pathetic "how could my husband do this to me" way that made my heart go out to this woman whom I barely even knew. I moved the rest of the way into the room and sat down on the edge of the bed. I may have hardly known her, but she had made every effort to make sure that I felt welcomed and comfortable in my new surroundings, and I felt that I owed her some compassion. She moved her head slightly and looked up at me for the first time since I'd come in.

"He left me, Tessa. I got up this morning and he had his suitcase packed, and he told me it was over." She started crying again as she spoke, so I gingerly put my hand on her head and smoothed back her hair, just as my mother had done for me back in high school. It's funny how we learn these things.

"Did he say why? Were you two having problems?" Another dumb question. I mean, the man had asked me to play Twister while his wife was in the ladies room.

"He...he said," she took a deep breath and bit her bottom lip, " he said there's someone else. He has a *girlfriend*, Tessa. That's where he went, did you know? He went to her house, to stay at his *girlfriend's* house. Probably some stripper slut from The Jiggly Kitty."

The words Jiggly Kitty triggered something inside my brain and I suddenly remembered the reason I had gone over there in the first place. I looked at my watch. 11:15.

Shit.

"Um, Kendra," I said, twisting one of her curls around my finger. "I hate to bring this up right now, but I actually barged into your house because the guys were worried about you missing your eleven o'clock with Rob."

"Rob can go to Hell," she said, turning over onto her side.

"Yes, well, that's definitely an option." I respectfully held back a giggle as I wasn't completely sure she was kidding. "Let me just make a phone call so they'll know you're not coming."

I stepped out into the hallway and called the office. Roberta put me on hold while she pulled either Chris or Dan from what was likely the worst meeting of their lives. When I heard Chris's voice pick up the phone I wished I had better news.

"Are you serious?" Chris asked. "Tessa, the man is about to rip us limb from limb. He doesn't care if I had a 3.95 GPA in college, he thinks my drawings suck."

"3.95?" I asked, trying to lighten the mood. "You didn't feel like going for the full 4.0?"

"I didn't want to seem unapproachable. Now tell me what the hell is wrong with Kendra?"

"I can't explain right now," I said. I didn't feel right announcing Kendra's marital problems to her coworkers after only working with her for her one week. "She's okay, but she's having a bit of an emotional crisis. I'm probably going to stay here for a while to keep her company."

"It's Todd isn't it?" asked Chris.

"I really can't say," I said. "But, you know, you've met the guy..."

"Oh, Jesus. Couldn't he have timed this better?"

"Look, just call my cell if you need anything. I really should get back in there to check on her."

"I will," said Chris. "I'd better get back in there too, or else Dan's going to be having an emotional crisis of his own."

I apologized about fifty-seven more times before hanging up. I wished that it had been Dan who answered the phone. For some reason giving Chris that kind of news made me feel awful, especially since I knew he was subconsciously blaming everything on the secretary. I threw my phone into my purse and headed back to Kendra's room.

"The worst part," she said, picking right up where she'd left off, "is that I didn't even see it coming. The thought never even crossed my mind, you know?" She blew her nose and threw the tissue to the floor.

I honestly didn't know. I mean, I'd met the man for five

minutes and could have told her that he was a cheating dirt bag. How could she not have seen it? Kara once dated a guy she met at the bar we hung out at after work. The first night they met he had been fired from his job, and for the duration of their six month relationship he failed to find another one. He made fun of the rest of us for being "working class suckers," and borrowed money off of her practically from their first date. For six months she rolled her eyes and said "Men!" whenever she spoke of his situation, as if all men on earth were useless bums. Nothing I said would convince her that there were good men, *better* men, out there, because who was I to judge? I didn't even have one myself. But I knew they existed. Megan Trask had managed to sink her hooks into one, hadn't she?

"You don't need him, Kendra," I said, ready to preach to a captive audience. I took off my heels and climbed into the bed beside her. God it was comfortable. "Look at you - you're young, you're beautiful, you're a successful engineer. Pretty soon he's going to realize he's made the biggest mistake of his life. But you know what? It won't even matter, because you'll have a hundred better guys lined up at your door like five minutes from now."

Right on cue, the doorbell rang.

"What did I tell you?" I said, climbing back off the bed. " Go put on something cute and I'll let them in."

Unfortunately, it was only the gardener from across the street standing on the doorstep and not the brigade of Marines that I had promised Kendra. He had come over to make sure everything was okay, and looked a little disappointed when I assured him that we were both just fine. I sent him on his way and wandered into the kitchen to make some tea, and also to do some gawking. Sunshine poured in through the kitchen skylights and I looked in awe through the sliding glass door and into the backyard. The swimming pool blended into the landscaping, nestled amongst rocks and palm trees and other tropical looking vegetation. Sunlight sparkled off the water. A large grill and full sized bar was set up on the patio, and I could see Christmas lights strung along the fence. It reminded me of a resort I had once been to in Jamaica, except this was where Kendra *lived*.

A vision of myself, scraping ice from my windshield on a February morning, left me with such a stark comparison that I moved from the window, literally shaking my head to clear the image before it became unbearable. I had gone into the kitchen to find some tea, not to wallow in self pity. There was a woman upstairs in a much worse situation than myself, regardless of how much money she had, and I should be thankful that at least for the moment my life was good.

I made two cups of tea and brought them upstairs along with two boxes of Girl Scout Cookies that I spotted on the counter. Kendra had made some progress while I was gone. She had moved into an upright position and was no longer staring listlessly at the ceiling.

"For you," I said, placing the tea on her bedside table. "And for us." I shook the boxes of Girl Scout cookies and climbed back into bed next to her with a pile of napkins.

I bit into a peanut butter patty and thought that maybe a change of subject might raise Kendra's spirits. I asked her about the paintings that I had noticed in her office and over the fireplace. She told me that against her parents wishes, she had been an art major during her freshman year of college. Though being the only child of Sean Flamhauser, and future heir to the company, she gave in to the pressure after only one semester and switched to a major in civil engineering. With all the talk from her friends and teachers about how difficult it might be to find a job after graduation, it seemed the only logical choice.

College was also where she had met her husband Todd. They were married shortly after graduation and moved to Las Vegas where her father set her up as Branch Manager. Todd had been provided with a comfortable position as Director of Business Development, but as of this morning she believed he had abandoned his job along with his marriage.

I told her that I too had been an art major, but saw it through to the end and had the dusty diploma hanging in my mom's basement to prove it. I told her about my love of turning what most people perceived as garbage into things of beauty. And I told her, with sadness, that the only art I had created lately was made out of paperclips and pushpins. She laughed and told me she had a nervous habit of folding origami paper cranes out of anything she could get her hands on. She picked one of the tissues up off the bed. It was hard to make out, but there it was, a wet, droopy pink crane.

Despite her tangled hair and tear-streaked face, she looked happier when she talked about art than when she was all glammed up discussing business. I no longer felt like I was alone in thinking that there was more to life than pushing paper. If this rich, successful, woman was not even satisfied with the life she had chosen, then I, in my position as glorified slave, had every right to feel the same.

At twelve-thirty Kendra silently stood up, walked over to a large bureau, and opened the bottom drawer. She grabbed a stack of boxer shorts - apparently where Todd had gone he didn't need underwear - and without a word, tossed them out the bedroom window. At one o'clock we watched Days of our Lives, which turned out to be both of our favorite soaps, and ate ice cream straight from the carton. At two o'clock we cut Todd out of several hundred photographs, and at three-thirty we took the pile of smiling Todd faces and burned them on the back porch.

Years worth of female bonding was forged in a matter of hours. It was four o'clock, and we were back in front of the television, when I decided that I had better return to the office to make sure that Chris and Dan hadn't set the building on fire. I dreaded facing them.

Kendra thanked me for staying with her and then apologized for being, as she put it, a blubbering ball of shit.

"All in a day's work," I said, handing her the remote control. "And the only ball of shit around here has his entire collection of underwear out on your front lawn. Call me if you need anything okay?"

"Please come back after work," she said. She flipped through the channels and landed on a woman in short shorts and a flabby gut screaming about paternity tests. "We'll eat pizza and ice cream for dinner."

I assured her that I would come back, and then stepped outside into the late afternoon sun. It felt like I had been away for days. I plucked a pair of green boxer shorts off the antennae of my car, and headed back to work.

***

Chris and Dan looked like they had been through a war.

"I kid you not, Rob told me, and I quote, 'if any of you ever pull this kind of shit again, I will pull the entire Jiggly Kitty account and your company can burn in Hell'," said Chris. " I swear to God he said that. I feared for my life, Tessa. Dan and I both did."

"We were almost holding hands under the table," said Dan. "From the terror."

"Aw, I'm sorry! But I brought you a little something to help make up for it." Their faces lit up when I returned from my office with two large Starbucks iced coffees. Bringing in coffee from the outside world is a huge deal to office workers - it's like smuggling drugs to a prisoner.

"You are the best secretary ever," said Chris. "Can we keep you?"

God was I relieved to hear him say those words.

"I'd love to," I said. "But not if Rob Dorfman is going to be around here all the time."

"Rob who?" asked Dan, taking a long sip of coffee and lounging back in his chair.

"That guy," said Chris, stirring his coffee with a straw, "can go to Hell."

Dan rolled over to the television and popped in a video game. "Come on Tessa, there'll be no more work taking place in this office today. Let's see how you do with some Mortal Kombat. Chris can play winner."

He handed me a controller and I settled into one of the video game chairs. I wasn't particularly a fan of Mortal Kombat, but it had been an interesting day, and I was ready to fight.

10

I watched the white plastic disc sail past Chris's hand and slide, with a satisfying clink, into the goal.

"Score!" I yelled. Several fifth graders turned to watch my victory dance.

"You realize that I lose on purpose so you'll continue to do that dance?" asked Chris. We pushed our paddles into the center of the table and headed toward the exit, casually bumping shoulders.

"I don't believe you. But it is an awesome dance and I wouldn't blame you if you did."

Chris and I were at the arcade where we had been hanging out during our lunch hour for the past week. It began the day after the Rob Dorfman meeting fiasco. Dan had pretty much given up on life and called in sick, taking the day to recover in front of the television. And Kendra, understandably, had decided to take the rest of the entire week off. I called to check on her periodically throughout the morning, but by eleven-thirty she seemed to be on some sort of cleaning rampage and I decided to just let her be. This left Chris and I alone in our corner of the office fielding phone calls and picking up the slack.

By noontime Chris declared that the only way to take his stress level down a notch would be with a game of air hockey. It took a good ten minutes before I realized he was serious, but when I did, I happily tagged along. Our business attire made us stick out like sore thumbs among the tourists and grade school children, but it also added to the silliness. I ended up having more fun than I'd had in a long time, and we have been going back ever since. We liked to laugh about the fact that people like Roberta, who saw us leave for lunch together everyday, probably thought we were having some kind of torrid affair.

We ordered two slices of pizza from the outdoor vendor, and took a seat on our favorite bench which overlooked the bumper boats. Making fun of passengers on the bumper boats was quickly becoming our favorite past time.

"Look at that kid," said Chris pointing to a boy, around twelve, who was making his boat repeatedly spin in circles. "He thinks he's the first one to figure out how to do that."

I laughed and pointed to the same kid's dad who was reaching into the water and splashing strangers in the face. "I would punch that guy if he splashed me."

"He's gonna get kicked out by bumper boat security," said Chris. "I can't wait." Sure enough, a pimply sixteen year old blew a whistle and Splash Dad was ordered out of the pool. His son looked humiliated.

"Look, now his kid's ramming the hell out of that other kid because he's angry at his dad," said Chris. "We could do a case study on this family."

"A case study?"

"I minored in psychology."

"You should write a research paper," I said. "And maybe you could also answer the question of why that guy over there is wearing green socks with sandals and black shorts."

"That one's simple. He's not concerned with fashion. He put those socks on because he needed something to cover his feet. And he put the sandals on because they're comfortable."

"And the shorts?" I asked.

"It's hot outside and those keep him cool. A guy like that doesn't think about color coordination or style, he thinks about putting clothes on his body for utilitarian purposes only."

"But how gross," I said. "His socks are all wet."

"Tessa, the guy is hanging out by himself at the bumper boats. Do you think he cares if his socks are wet? He's in his own little world, and he's probably much happier than the rest of us materialistic jerks."

"Are you materialistic?" I asked, looking up at him with a serious face. "You don't seem that way to me."

"Maybe not with brand name clothes, but come on, look at my office. And what do I do all day? I help some sociopath make money off of his strip joints. This entire city is the most materialistic piece of work on the planet. You go out on a Friday night around here and it's nothing but fake girls in thousand dollar shoes latching on to whoever has the most money, and lining up for the most exclusive clubs they can pay their way into."

"Geez," I said. "I was kind of hoping to hit up some clubs one of these weekends, but maybe I'd better go shoe shopping first. You know, if I want to catch a man."

"Your shoes are perfect," said Chris, playfully stepping on my foot. I cringed as I noticed the scuff marks all over the toes. How the heck old were these things?

"You don't want to be like those girls anyway," he said. He reached down and brushed some pizza crumbs off my leg. "They don't have any interest in air hockey."

I smiled up at him, and then looked quickly back down at my pizza. Perhaps it was the Las Vegas sun, but my face suddenly felt very warm. I stared at Splash Dad as he kicked angrily at the bushes by the bumper boat waiting area. A woman wearing a lot of gold jewelry hurried over to comfort him. Splash Mom, I assumed.

"So," I said, changing the subject, "not that I don't enjoy it, but we always seem to be making fun of other people or talking about work. I still don't know very much about you. There's got to be more to you than just designer of strip club parking lots and air hockey phenomenon, no?"

"Well, when you put it that way, could there possibly be anything more?"

I giggled. "Let me rephrase that. Once we get past all the glamour, there must be something that brought you to this point in your life. I can tell you quite simply that I was born and raised in Massachusetts, have hated the snow ever since I got too old to play in it, and have a very real fear of dying an administrative assistant. Now you go."

"First of all, you're never too old to play in the snow," said Chris.

"Tell me," I said, "have you ever had to scrape ice off your windshield before leaving for work on a ten degree February morning?"

"No, but once when I was six we took a ski trip to Colorado and I think my parents had to brush some snow off the car," said Chris. "But, you know, I was all snug in the back seat with the heat on."

"Exactly. I don't want to hear about snow from you, Mr. I Live In The Desert."

"Touché. But I haven't always lived in the desert. I grew up in San Diego and went to UCLA for my engineering degree. Right before graduation my roommates and I decided that before we sold our souls to the corporate world we wanted to do something for ourselves. So we moved to Vegas and tried our hand at amateur pornography."

I wish I could have seen the look on my face, because Chris only lasted about three seconds before he broke out laughing.

"I'm just kidding! Believe it or not we opened a paintball field, but it tanked. I don't think any of us had the drive or the experience to make it a success. But we had fun while it lasted."

We watched as Splash Dad made it loudly known to everybody who passed him that he would never frequent these bumper boats again.

"Do you still talk to the other guys?" I asked.

"I do. Randy is still my roommate. The other guy, Ryan, met a producer of Cirque du Soleil when we were out at the bars one night. He ended up marrying the girl and now he travels the world. Every few months I get a postcard from some new country that he's in."

"Well there you go," I said. "Every decision you make, no matter how insignificant it seems, can change the direction of your entire life. I mean, what if he hadn't gone out that night? He'd probably still be here like the rest of us corporate chumps."

"True, true." Chris nodded slowly. "And if you hadn't carried a tube of stain remover in your purse, you may have never ended up in Vegas at all."

"Exactly. And if Kendra's husband hadn't left, she never would have missed her meeting with Rob, Rob never would have tore you a new one, and we may never have ended up hanging out at this arcade together like a couple of dorks." I kicked him gently under the bench.

"Now that would be a shame."

We watched in silence as Splash Dad put his son in a headlock and administered one hell of a noogie.

"I'm guessing that guy never thinks about these things," said Chris.

"Good call."

***

We made a stop at the arcade gift shop before returning to the office as we still had a few precious minutes left of our lunch hour. We wound our way up and down the aisles laughing at the miscellaneous junk for sale. You could pretty much slap a pair of googly eyes on anything and sell it in one of these places. We had just finished giggling over a pink t-shirt emblazoned with several hundred kittens and, of course, the words 'Las Vegas,' when something caught my eye.

"Hey look at these," I called to Chris, picking one up. It

was a small sculpture made from pieces of junk metal, nuts, bolts, and various other parts. The one I had picked up looked like a dog with its head in a toilet. "This is kind of cool, huh?"

"Not bad," he said. "You were an art major right?"

"Sure was," I said. "I used to make stuff like this." I turned the dog around in my hand, studying it. It wasn't anything that I couldn't have made myself. The tag told me it was made by a woman in Carson City who worked out of a studio in her home - and she was charging thirty-two dollars. Boy was I jealous.

"So you don't anymore?" asked Chris. "Make stuff like that, I mean."

"Not really. I have to concentrate on my *career* you know." I stuck my tongue out at him. "Typing, filing. Once you let creativity into the mix you're just asking for trouble."

"You should try to get back into it. I tell you, the year and a half we spent running paintball was the best time I've had since college."

"Well I haven't totally given up on it. I still make things out of office supplies sometimes. Usually when I'm on hold with Jiggly Kitty tech support."

"Office supplies?"

"That's right. I made the Eiffel Tower out of binder clips."

"You're kidding."

"Nope." I put on a leopard print cowboy hat. "What do you think?"

"I think that hat has been on more heads than you realize. What else have you made?"

I tossed him the hat and did a little skip down the next aisle. "Uh, oh yeah. Before I left I was starting to work on a diorama of *Dogs Playing Poker*."

"Out of office supplies."

"Yup. It's hard to find the right stuff though with stupid Margaret Sherman always nosing around when I'm in the supply closet. What do you think of *this*?" I put on a pair of battery operated sunglasses. Red and blue lights chased each other around the frames, and Chris snapped a picture with his cell phone. I smelled his cologne as he moved in close and plucked the sunglasses from my face.

"I think," he said, looking into my eyes, "you're hiding a lot of talent from the world."

***

I started sculpting as soon as we returned to the office. With my door closed, a pack of sticky notes, a box of paperclips, some pushpins, and various other items I snagged out of the supply closet when Roberta had gone to the bathroom, I set to work. At three-thirty I stood in Chris's doorway and proudly presented him with a tiny air hockey table and two tiny players, all secured atop a green file folder.

"For you," I said. "It's us."

The look on his face when he saw my work was priceless.

"You weren't kidding." He whistled. "This is unbelievable. I shall give this a place of honor."

Chris rolled his chair over to the windowsill and placed my sculpture in the center, reminding me of Nick on the day I left Massachusetts. For the first time all day I felt a little sad. Then Chris pulled a dog sculpture made out of nuts and bolts from beneath his desk - the one that he had probably purchased while I was in the gift shop's restroom - and my heart skipped a beat.

"I thought you could use this," he said with a wink. "For inspiration."

"You're something else, you know that?" I said. I took the little dog out of his hands and smiled the whole way back to my office.

11

Sophisticated slutty. I stood in Kendra's doorway twirling my hair and turning the words over in my head. My mind ran through all of the outfits that I had brought from home, and they all seemed so lame. I mean, I could definitely pull off slutty if I mixed the right pieces together, but sophisticated? Not a chance.

"Tessa? You okay?" asked Kendra, snapping me back to reality.

"Exactly how hot are we talking?" I asked. I suddenly remembered what Chris had told me about phony girls and thousand dollar shoes and boob jobs. Did he really say boob jobs? I glanced down at my chest and panic started to set in again. "Are you sure you want to hang out with me tonight?"

I had assumed that Kendra had loads of rich and exciting girlfriends who she hung out with, so when I found myself invited to accompany her to one of the newest clubs on The Strip, I was more than a little surprised.

"Of course I want to go with *you*, silly, who else?" She effortlessly swished her hair up into a clip and I wondered what on earth somebody like Kendra wanted with somebody like me. Little, old, secretarial me.

Just as I was surprised to find myself being flown to Vegas after merely helping her remove a stain from her dress, I was equally surprised to find myself suddenly elevated from the position of assistant to the position of somebody worth hanging out with. But this was the new Kendra, the one who returned to the office. She was truly a changed woman. No longer depressed and moping, she was full of life and spirit, ready to head out on the town and revel in the fact that she was once again a single woman. I was not quite sure how that change had happened, but as I'd yet to experience much of Vegas nightlife, I was too excited to care.

There was just one minor catch. In order to actually get into this club, we had to look really good. Not trashy, as Kendra explained it, but "sophisticated slutty." Being a hot girl is a sure ticket into the Vegas club scene, and I did not want to let Kendra down.

Kendra must have finally noticed the worried look forming on my face because she suggested that we go shopping during lunch, and I eagerly accepted.

We drove to shops at The Venetian where Kendra marched me straight into several of her favorite stores. These were the types of stores I would never dream of going into by myself - where there are four racks of clothing and the employees stand at the entrance judging your worth. But it was different walking in with Kendra. Some of the employees knew her by name, and instead of looking at me like I was a hillbilly, they assumed that I belonged.

"I don't know if I can afford this stuff, Ken," I whispered, getting nervous when I spotted the price tag on a mini-skirt. I would have to work ten hours to pay for that thing. No, I take that back, I would have to work ten hours just to pay for the front half of that thing. If I felt like walking around bare-assed tonight we'd be in business.

"Oh don't worry about money," said Kendra, holding a purple sequined tube top up against me. Almost everything in the store was purple. "I'm the one dragging you out tonight, I'll take care of your outfit."

As much as I didn't want to let her buy me any more stuff, there were so many beautiful things in the store that I figured I would let it slide this one last time. The clerk eagerly brought several items to the dressing room for me, and I got the distinct impressions that we were the only customers she'd seen all day. I cringed at the price tag on the mini dress I was slipping into, and prayed that nothing ripped as I zipped up.

All concerns about money disappeared when I saw the person looking back at me from the mirror. She was nobody I had ever met before - she was rich, she was glowing, she was ready to mingle with celebrities! I had to have it. Kendra and the store clerk both gasped when I stepped out of the dressing room. This dress had "sophisticated slutty" and Tessa Golden written all over it.

"We'll take it," said Kendra nodding approvingly. "Now we just need to get you some stilettos."

The fact that I was going to be seen in public in a dress that short barely had time to sink in, and now we were talking about stilettos?

"Do they sell mace in this mall?" I asked, only half joking. I went back into the dressing room and reluctantly took off my heavenly new dress.

Kendra just laughed.

"Don't worry, you'll blend right in."

***

And blend in I did. We stood in line outside the club with at least a hundred other girls dressed just like us, or worse. The amount of skin was shocking and I elbowed Kendra every six seconds.

"Look at *her*!" I whispered as a girl walked by in a dress that barely grazed the bottom of her behind. I looked around at the men, trying to figure out what was going through their minds. The sad part is that most of them did not even seem phased, as if they were desensitized to seeing that amount of skin. I guess they had to be, otherwise they would have a heart attack every time they turned around. But it made me wonder what went on inside the clubs to keep them interested. Before I had a chance to ponder it further, a bouncer motioned for Kendra and I to come to the front of the line. Several girls gave us filthy looks.

"How are we doing tonight ladies?" asked the bouncer, checking our ID's. "Right this way." He unlatched the red velvet rope and we rode up the escalator to the club entrance, looking down on the less fortunate people who, Kendra informed me, might be waiting there all night.

As good as I looked, I take no credit whatsoever for our being chosen from the crowd. Men who did not give a second look to the countless scantily clad women who walked by literally stopped mid-sentence when Kendra was in the area. Thigh high white boots and a black mini-dress certainly contributed, but she would have done just as well in a potato sack.

We hadn't even made it across the room to the bar when two men practically got into a fist fight over who was going to buy us a drink.

"Boys, boys," said Kendra, "we'll be here all night, everybody will get their chance." We settled into a plush green couch overlooking the dance floor and toasted each other with our first round of drinks. It's not like I've never had a man buy me a drink before, but this was nuts.

"Let's play a game," shouted Kendra over the noise. "It's called Who Would You Do? Heard of it?"

I laughed. "Oh yes, it's a classic!"

"Okay good, you go first!"

I told her that my number one pick would always and forever be Nick Trask. Kendra did not know Nick, but I assured her of his do-ability. She argued that I had to pick someone from the Las Vegas branch. I really wanted to pick Chris, as he is cute in his own way, when his glasses slip down his nose while he leans over his desk, and the way he kind of stinks at air hockey. But I did not want her to get the wrong idea about us, so instead I chose Dan.

"Really?" asked Kendra. "I would have guessed Chris."

When Kendra chose Phil Baxter, the forty-something draftsman from the 30th floor who looks like he's done a lot of drugs in his lifetime and smells of cigarettes and whiskey, I choked on my drink. She couldn't explain to me what it was about him, but ever since the day she denied his vacation request and he brazenly told her to go to Hell, she couldn't keep her eyes off of him. Phil was a bad boy with a steady job - the perfect compromise for the rich girl with a warped version of slumming.

"You know," she said. "I'm single now. Maybe I should go for it and put the moves on ol' Phil."

"Phil's married," I said. "Plus, there's a little thing called sexual harassment in the workplace, remember?"

"Blah blah blah!" she shouted over the music, making a pouty face. "You'll never get anywhere in life with that attitude!"

Maybe she was right. Maybe I was too worried about what was right and what was wrong. Maybe I should just go for it once in a while. Suddenly my cell phone felt as if it was burning a hole in my purse. I took it out and stared at Nick's name in my list of Contacts while Kendra peered over my shoulder. I was just about to text him something witty, something life-changing, when I could have sworn that Justin Timberlake walked in the main entrance. By the time Kendra and I finished arguing over whether or not it was really him, we had drained our martinis and each done a shot of tequila.

My phone was long forgotten at the bottom of my purse as we headed onto the dance floor. By that time I was sufficiently drunk enough to consider dancing, and the music was irresistible. We pushed our way to the center, through the gyrating bodies, and found ourselves a few square feet to dance in. In a matter of seconds we had attracted a swarm of heinous looking men approaching from all sides, acting as if it were purely coincidence that we were in the path of their sweaty, pulsating, loins. One of them snuck up from behind and put his hand around my waist. Kendra gently pulled me toward her and we inched away towards safer territory.

A cute guy in a black button-up shirt caught my eye. He wasn't dancing with anybody in particular, just moving his head to the music and surveying the crowd. I stared at him for a few seconds until he looked my way, then I took a sip of my beer and gave him a smile. I looked away as he moved closer. I didn't want to appear *too* interested. He circled my area for about ten minutes as I alternated between flirty smiles and the cold shoulder. Finally he was right there in front of me when one of my favorite songs came on.

"Whooo!" I shouted holding my beer up in the air. Somebody's flailing elbow caught me in the back and shoved me directly into him. He caught me on his chest and I remained there for the rest of the song, dancing in ways that would have made my grandmother roll over in her grave. I was pretty drunk and before I knew it I was making out with this guy whose name I didn't know and, to be honest, had no interest in finding out.

"I'm going to get some more drinks!" I shouted when I finally came up for air.

"I'll go with you!" he shouted back. Up close he looked a little bit like a Muppet. As he followed me to the bar I realized with a jolt of panic that Kendra wasn't on the dance floor anymore. I looked over to the couch where we had been sitting and, to my horror, there she was, dancing on top of the cocktail table surrounded by men. I don't know if she owned a training video or what, but she had some very Jiggly Kitty-like moves down cold.

"That's my friend!" I shouted at black shirt Muppet guy. "I should probably get her down from there!" He followed me over to the table where I tapped Kendra on the bottom of her boot.

"Whooo!" she yelled when she saw me, and tried to pull me up onto the table with her.

"You're going to fall!" I screamed back and motioned for her to come down. Reluctantly she slid off the table, and a few of the men gave me dirty looks for ruining their fun.

"Have some class," I told them as we stumbled over to the bar for more beers. I seemed to have lost black shirt Muppet guy in the process, which was totally fine, so we danced our way back onto the dance floor alone. My feet were killing me but the strobe lights and the driving music kept me going for another hour.

"Let's go to the ladies room!" I finally shouted into Kendra's ear. We made our way to the restroom and I plopped down on a toilet seat, not caring about germs, only thinking that this was the most fun I'd ever had in my life. I pulled my phone out of my purse. A lipstick fell out as well and rolled under the stalls.

"Nooo!" I screeched, lunging for the lipstick and peeing a little bit on the floor. I cracked up laughing as Kendra kicked it back to me.

"What are you *doing* in there?" she asked. Her voice was scratchy.

"Texting somebody," I said. And I was. At that moment, on the toilet, I wanted nothing more than to tell Nick how hot I thought he was. I needed to take some chances in my life. If Kendra didn't care that Phil Baxter was married, why should I let those things bother me?

u r SOG

u r ROT

u r HOG

I was having some trouble typing.

u r HOT

Finally I got the letters right and hit send.

"Oh my God, I sent it!" I kicked the stall door open so hard that it swung back and smashed into the one next to it. "Oops!"

"You're insane!" Kendra slid down the wall laughing hysterically.

I washed my hands and took a paper towel from the bathroom attendant who I could tell, even in my drunken state, found us to be beyond obnoxious.

"I can't believe I just sent that!" We pushed through the restroom door and fell onto the closest couch we could find. In less than one minute my phone began vibrating. Kendra grabbed it and held it up over her head out of my reach.

"No! Let go!" I jumped up and tried to grab it but instead tripped over her foot and fell down onto my knees laughing.

Kendra clamped a hand over her mouth. "Are you okay? I didn't mean to almost kill you." She pulled me back onto the couch. "And careful of that dress, you don't want to give anybody a free show."

I pulled my dress down as far as I could, which wasn't far.

"Look who's talking Miss Dances on Tables. How the hell did you end up there anyway?"

"You were busy sucking face with that guy who looks like Kermit. I got bored." She shrugged and tossed the phone onto my lap. I opened it up.

u r not so bad yourself

"He says I'm not so bad myself!" I shoved the phone into her face so she could see. She snatched it back out of my hand.

"Let me reply!" She started typing like crazy and holding the phone out of my reach again.

"What did you say? What did you say?"

"I asked him what he's wearing."

"You did not!" I threw my head against the back of the couch and slid down to the floor. "I just died of embarrassment."

Within thirty seconds the phone vibrated again and I told Kendra to just read it to me as I couldn't bear to look.

"He said '*use your imagination*'."

"Give me that!" I took the phone back and starting typing. Kendra watched over my shoulder.

careful what u wish for big boy

"What the heck does that even mean?" she asked.

"I have no idea," I said, laughing and falling over onto my side.

i'm wishing u weren't so far away right now, wrote back Nick.

oh please, I wrote, *u wouldn't be able 2 handle me*

"Are you crazy?" yelled Kendra, ripping the phone out of

my hands. "You are not allowed to send anymore texts tonight!" She was just about to push the power button when one last message came through from Nick.

"What's it say, what's it say?" I asked, bouncing up and down on the couch.

Kendra shook her head back and forth in mock disgust.

"He said, *u wanna bet?*" She hit the power button and threw my phone into her purse. "That's it! Nighty-night text messaging. No phone for you!"

"Aw, but Ken, you have no idea how hot this guy is!" I whined. "If he wants to make a bet I shouldn't let him down!"

"No more!"

"Fine," I said. "But you know what we do need more of?"
"What's that?"

"Shots!"

We stumbled back toward the bar, laughing our asses off, and I remember no more of that night.

12

I am so sorry about last night. With butterflies in my stomach I punched the words into my phone and quickly hit Send.

It was 9:00 a.m. on Friday morning, and my hangover was the least of my reasons for feeling sick. I had woken up on the floor of my hotel room, not completely sure how I got there, but with the unpleasant realization that I needed to get ready for work. Thursday night drinking is cool when you're in college, but out here in the real world it is one of the worst ideas ever. I heaved myself off the floor and grabbed my phone out of my purse, which had somehow been slung on top of the microwave.

"Why the heck is my phone off?" I wondered out loud. A few seconds after turning it back on, a new text message came through. It was from Nick, from 12:18 a.m. the night before.

What say we find out? it read.

"What does that mean?" I mumbled to myself. Then, with increasing horror, I scrolled back through the prior night's conversation. "Oh my God...no....." I clamped a hand over my mouth and tried not to hyperventilate.

I kept reading the words over and over again - all my secret feelings for Nick laid out there in horrific text message grammar. I sent off the apology text as soon as my hands stopped shaking, and took the phone with me into the bathroom while I showered. But by the time I had finished getting ready I still hadn't received a reply from Nick. With my head hanging in shame, and a bag of McDonald's greasiest hangover cure on the passenger seat, I drove into work.

I stopped in the lobby to tell Charlene about what had just gone down, but was quickly interrupted by the arrival of Fartz the Fed Ex guy dropping packages all over the place.

"Ugh," said Charlene. "Just get upstairs, run while you can."

I hurried past Roberta, trying to avoid making bloodshot eye contact, and slipped into my office. I was just about to start checking emails when Chris popped into my doorway. He studied me curiously with one eyebrow raised.

"How you feeling?" he asked, taking a seat on the other side of my desk.

"I'm good, good. Really good," I said. I spread my Egg McMuffin and Hash Brown out on the desk and took a bite of each, letting the warm greasy goodness work its magic. "Why do you ask?"

"You just look a little tired, like you were out late." He gave me a sympathetic smile while at the same time shaking his head in disapproval. "You feel like hitting the arcade today?"

"I'm sorry, Chris," I said. "But I think I need to spend my lunch hour napping in the car today. Rain check?"

"No problem. You sure you're okay?" He eyed my

breakfast. "Need me to get you a Croissan'wich or something?"

"Very funny," I said. "But I'm fine, really. Kendra was just reliving her youth last night. Celebrating her divorce. And me being her new best friend, I guess I've just got to learn to keep up." I shrugged, because really, I didn't have any idea how it had all happened either. "Marisa will be back before you know it, and then this will be her problem anyway."

At the mention of Marisa returning from maternity leave, Chris gave a sad smile and nodded slowly, looking down at his hands.

"That is, you know, unless Kendra begs me to stay here," I added quickly. I gave Chris what I hoped was a reassuring smile and self-consciously ran my fingers through my hair. I had been having such a good time in Las Vegas that the idea of actually leaving in a few months hadn't occurred to me, nor had the thought that certain people might prefer me to stay. I mean, certain people had only known each other for a few weeks. We sat in somewhat awkward silence for a good ten seconds. Chris was the first to break it.

"People around the office are starting to talk," he said, changing the subject. "They want to know what really happened with Kendra. She's going to have to release some kind of official statement."

Chris and Dan were the only two people I had told about Todd. Everybody else was living off of the rumors that started when he stopped showing up to work. For the most part they had figured out that the marriage was over, but jealous women liked to place the blame on Kendra. They assumed that she was the one who cheated, and even if they did allow the possibility that it was Todd, they figured that Kendra had driven him to it. They delighted in the thought that she was finally turning into the train wreck they always suspected her to be. I was starting to hate every single one of them.

"It's really nobody's business but her own. If she doesn't want to share her personal life with ev..." I trailed off when I saw an email pop into my Inbox - from Nick. My heart started pounding and I knew I couldn't possibly wait for Chris to leave before I read it, so I just tuned him out.

Hey you...no worries about last night. I must say I rather enjoyed it ;) I spent the night on the couch drinking and watching Hoarders...this woman had cat shit under her mattress, no joke. Anyway, Megan said I work too much...stay out too late with clients...blah blah blah...like I have a choice? Not like she isn't out three nights a week with her greasy lawyer friends. At least when I'm out I'm working. Sort of. Anyway, maybe it's my hangover talking, but I can't stop thinking about you. Come back home or I quit, I swear I'll do it. - N

" - never seen so many wizards gathered in one place before."

"Huh?" I asked. I hadn't heard a word Chris was yammering about. Something about wizards? Really, it's things like that that explain why he doesn't have a girlfriend.

"I knew you weren't listening to me," he said. "What are you reading?"

"Nothing, just an email from a friend." My mind was racing. Nick couldn't stop thinking about me! He was having problems with Megan. I needed to send a reply. Why wouldn't Chris get the hell out of my office?

"Well, you enjoy that," said Chris. He gave me a defeated

wave and sauntered back to his office. I felt momentarily guilty as I heard the air squish sadly out of the soft padding of his desk chair.

But this email from Nick, this email was monumental. It was the first time I had heard directly from him that there was trouble with his marriage. Kara had mentioned, the last time we spoke, that Nick was having her transfer calls from his wife directly into voicemail, a sign that things may not be as peachy as they appeared. But I never felt that it was my place to bring the subject up.

Though now, not only did he tell me, but he combined it with how much he missed me, and how much he enjoyed our naughty little text-capades last night. Not to say that I would ever *do* anything with a married man, as I do have respect for the institution. But there is nothing in the bible about not flirting with a married man via email, especially when you are safely situated three thousand miles away and have been crushing on this married man for three years. I kept this in mind as I started my reply.

Hey - I'm glad you're not freaked out, but I would still like to reiterate the fact that I was, how should I put it....obliterated last night? Whatever I said, you know I'd never say those things normally, or try to make things weird with us. Not that I don't think you're hot, or "sog," or whatever I may have called you ;) Sorry to hear about Megan...I could've told you marrying a foreclosure attorney was a bad idea.

I felt slightly guilty taking his side with no questions asked. I mean, I had met the woman one time and here I was passing judgment about what kind of a person she was. If I really thought about it I was no better than the women in my office who were judging Kendra. So I didn't think about it. Nick was my friend, and friends are supposed to support each other, right? Except that I took it one step further.

I know if I were your wife I would never make you sleep on the couch. In fact I may never let you leave the bed.

I swear to God that I only typed it to see what it looked like on the screen, like some kind of email version of Russian Roulette. I sat and stared at the words for a good thirty seconds. If I actually sent this email there would be no more hiding behind the excuse of being drunk. My words would be time-stamped clear as day -10:30 a.m. Friday morning - sent from my office email account to boot. I fully intended to delete it, I swear I did, when Kendra popped into my doorway and scared the life out of me. I quickly hit Send, and off it went.

I blinked stupidly at the screen as Kendra dropped off a ton of work for me to do for the Riverlin Zoning Commission filing. Today was the filing deadline and, as usual, everything at Flamhauser-Geist is left to the last minute.

I half-listened to her instructions while keeping one eye on my Inbox. What the hell had I been thinking? What was I trying to get myself into? When Kendra left I turned on my Dictaphone and tried to push thoughts of Nick Trask out of my mind, while a few not so innocent thoughts tried to push their way in. My stomach was in knots, and every time a little envelope icon appeared in my taskbar I had a couple of heart attacks. None of them were from Nick though, so I began typing up the cover letter Kendra had left for me. I forgot about my love life for a second as her voice read me the following sentence:

We believe that the project will not only bring revenue to this previously undeveloped part of the city, but will also create at least thirty-five new jobs.

I debated telling her that perhaps these were not the types of jobs that Riverlin was looking to create. It is hard to imagine that thanks to the mind numbingly boring work I do each day, a place like The Jiggly Kitty is able to exist. Everything is kitten themed down to the sign over the restroom that reads "Litter Boxes," which I find in extremely poor taste as there is absolutely nothing sexy about a litter box. There is also the demeaning bowl of imaginary milk built into the end of the stage which the girls are required to "lap up" before ending their performance. And rather than beckoning dancers to their side of the stage by waving dollar bills in the air, a long stick with feathers and tinsel at the end is handed to each patron as they enter the club. Welcome citizens of Riverlin! Your new careers await! It occurred to me as I was typing the letter that Rob Dorfman may have had some serious issues growing up.

Later in the afternoon Mike Halloran, our intern, appeared in my doorway with an armload of plans, ready to hit the road. He had exactly forty-five minutes to get to city hall before the four o'clock deadline, and Riverlin was approximately forty-seven minutes away.

I printed out my letter and told him to wait a second while I got Kendra's signature. Mike earned all of our respect a week ago when he got into a six car pileup on his way to Las Vegas City Hall. Without missing a beat, he fled the scene and made it there exactly one minute before they closed. He wedged his foot into the door, entering into a battle of strength with the city clerk, but Mike is a strong kid, and she reluctantly gave in.

Mike was later cited by the police for leaving the scene of an accident, but Flamhauser-Geist took care of the fine. It is that kind of dedication that our company appreciates, and in Mike they saw much promise. He was fresh blood. One more warm body willing to contribute to the degradation of one more American city.

I finally got an email reply from Nick who had been tied up in meetings for most of the day. When I read what it said my jaw nearly hit the floor, and me being a lady, that is all that I can tell you.

13

"I've got something for you," said Kendra. From behind her back she pulled a small framed painting and laid it on my desk. Two women sat at a bar, one in pink and one in lilac, both sipping on color coordinated martinis.

"For *me*?" I asked in awe. It was beautiful, and it matched my office perfectly. When on Earth she had time to do this was beyond me, as we had been hitting the clubs pretty hard over the past week.

"I painted it the other night, you know, the one that we didn't go out drinking. What was that, Monday?" She gave me a wink. "I know how much you liked the others. Think of it as a thank you gift."

"You don't need to make me presents!" I said. "I've been having a blast hanging out with you. I haven't been to so many bars in my entire life."

"Well good," she said, running her finger along the frame, "then you won't mind when I tell you that we're going out this weekend. And...." she paused for dramatic effect, "I've found us dates!" She giggled like a maniac and high-tailed it back to her office before I could even process what she had just said. *Dates?*

"Kendra!" I followed her into her office. "Dates? Are you serious? First of all, when and where on earth did you find us dates? Second, do I have any say in this?"

"I was grabbing lunch over at Finnegan's, right, and these two guys got in line behind me." She started unwrapping a humongous sandwich. Shredded lettuce sprinkled out onto her desk. "The shorter guy, he goes 'you have a really nice figure.' I mean who uses the word 'figure' anymore you know?" She plucked out pickles one by one and deposited them into a napkin.

"So far he sounds pretty creepy," I said, crinkling my nose. "How come you didn't just order that without pickles?"

"I was a little distracted. So I turned around to look at who said it, and that's when I noticed his friend." Her eyes lit up.

"His friend was Brad Pitt?"

"No, silly. His friend was Bryce Storm, male model turned Hollywood cosmetic dentist to the stars!"

I stared at her. I may have blinked a few times.

"Come on, *Bryce Storm.* He's done the teeth of half of Hollywood, he's a regular on *Why Am I Ugly?* You must know him."

I blinked a few more times.

Kendra rolled her eyes at me. "Well, anyway, they're hanging out at the MGM Grand Saturday night and asked me to join. I told them only if I could bring a friend, and of course they loved the idea."

"Of course they loved the idea, they're probably rapists!" All I could picture was a guy who told random women they had nice figures slipping me a roofie.

"They're not rapists, they're dentists. It'll be fine, it's not even really a *date.*" She rolled her eyes again. "I was exaggerating. We'll just meet them for a few drinks. If they turn out to be lame, we can lose them. At least we'll get some free drinks out of it." She toasted me with her Coca-Cola bottle.

"Who said I even want to go on a date? Maybe I'm seeing somebody, did you ever think of that?"

"Who? The married guy from back home? Come on Tess, I know you don't have a boyfriend."

"I'll have you know," I said, stabbing my finger in her direction, "that he is having trouble with his wife, and he *misses* me." I stuck out my tongue and went back into my office.

It was true. Ever since I accidentally sent that naughty email to Nick last week, we had been exchanging some pretty inappropriate emails and texts. And while I was enjoying it, I was also feeling a teensy bit guilty, which is something I never thought I would feel with Nick. I had always dreamed about the day he would arrive at my doorstep with a bouquet of roses and confess that it was me, that it had *always* been me, and everything in the universe would just fall into place.

Yet something felt off about the way things were going down. Maybe it was partly because I was still hanging out with Chris, and every time a naughty text message came in while we were playing air hockey, I told him it was from my mom.

"So come to my house at nine, okay?" Kendra shouted.

"And wear something cute!"

"Yeah, yeah," I answered. "Sophisticated slutty." I would be there, I couldn't let her meet these psychos by herself. An awful thought suddenly occurred to me and I ran back into her office. "Hey, if you're all over this Bryce guy, that means you're sticking me with the 'nice figure' creep aren't you?"

She took a conveniently huge bite out of her sandwich.

"Mmmphmmh." She pointed to her mouth and shrugged.

***

Kendra was already half in the bag when I picked her up on Saturday night. I found her puttering around behind the bar in her basement, sipping on a Long Island Iced Tea. The smell of her perfume hit me as soon as I walked in - it was definitely something by one pop star or another. She had really laid it on thick. Latin beats pumped out of the speakers that were stationed around the room, and a 56" plasma flat screen television hung on the wall across from the bar. Six bikini clad models were booty shaking into the camera.

"MTV, huh?" I raised an eyebrow. The girls were now gyrating from within a hot tub. There was a man in the tub too, but he had no teeth. I take that back, he had three teeth, all of which were gold. I tried to imagine running into that guy at the grocery store, and I wasn't so sure he could convince me to go back to his hot tub with him. This is why I haven't watched MTV since I was twenty-two. Something in my brain shut off on my twenty-third birthday and I just don't seem to get it anymore. Kendra, on the other hand, was thirty-two and loving it. Though I suspect the marital crisis she was going through had something to do with it.

"Look at those girls," said Kendra. "I look as good as them, right?" She turned to face the back of the bar and did a pretty terrible impersonation. I lost sight of her as she dipped down to the floor, but I did hear something crack.

"Of course you do," I said. "But maybe next time you should stretch first."

She stood up, rubbing her knee. "Remind me not to try that move again." She mixed another Long Island Iced Tea with a Playboy bunny stirrer and pushed it across the bar to me.

"No Jiggly Kitty stirrers?" I asked. "Where's your loyalty?"

Kendra laughed. "I used to have a bunch of Kitty stirrers, but they all broke. Cheap pieces of crap, Rob probably picked them out himself."

I took a sip of my drink and stared at the TV. The girls were now at some sort of bikini car wash, except two of them had gotten into the car, while the rest were just kind of squeezing soapy water all over themselves. The car wasn't getting too clean.

"So Todd called me today," said Kendra, out of no where. I tore myself away from the television and looked at her, this time with both eyebrows raised. As far as I knew she hadn't spoken to Todd since the day he left. The overdose of perfume and trashy music was starting to make sense.

"Oh no, what'd he want?" I asked.

"Just to tell me to expect the divorce papers by Fed Ex on Monday and that he'd really appreciate it if I would sign them ASAP. He actually said ASAP to me."

I didn't say anything as Kendra used the term ASAP quite

frequently around the office.

"He said that him and Carlotta, that's her name, *Carlotta,* just want to move on with their lives. Can you believe that? He leaves *me* and now he's acting like I'm keeping him from moving on with his precious life. If he wants me to sign the papers so badly, I'll *sign* the stupid papers. I would've driven to his lawyer's office today and signed them in person if I knew how God damned important it was to him. I certainly don't want to stand in the way of their happiness."

She had been moving all around behind the bar as she talked, picking up liquor bottles from one spot and slamming them down in another. But then she stopped, covered her mouth with her hand, and the next thing I knew she had sunk down to the floor behind the bar and was quietly sobbing.

"Oh Kendra, no, don't cry!" I walked behind the bar and sat down on the floor next to her. In front of us was a storage shelf lined with vodka, tequila, and countless mixers. A person couldn't have picked a better place for an emotional breakdown.

She laid her head on my shoulder and my arm grew wetter with each of her sobs. I could not think of what to say. All the breakups I had been through seemed so trivial and juvenile in comparison. I imagined Nick walking out on his wife to be with me. Is this what it would do to her? How horrible! How could I ever want to be the cause of this kind of pain? I felt sickened at the thought of the email I had last sent.

"Everything will be okay," I said at last, relying on the old standard. I became slightly braver and ventured on. "Signing those papers will be the best thing you've ever done, you know. And better that it happened now, instead of ten years down the road when you had kids and stuff. Besides, this whole house is *yours,* Ken. The house, the car, everything in it. Todd's nothing without you. He's screwed."

"Yeah, by Carlotta!" She burst into a fresh set of tears and sniffles. Something dripped onto my shoulder and she mopped it off me with a bar towel. "I'm sorry, look at me, I'm turning you into a soggy mess."

"It's okay," I said. "It's good to let it out. I knew something was up anyway when I saw the junk you were watching on TV." I pulled a bottle of raspberry vodka from the shelf and poured us two shots. "Here, let's have some of this." I raised my glass. "To your new life and our hot dates. You didn't forget about them did you?" She giggled and shook her head. Then we downed them.

Kendra wiped her eyes with the same bar towel she had used to mop the tears and snot off my shoulder. We stood up and brushed ourselves off.

"Ready?" I asked.

"Ready," said Kendra.

Two champagne glasses on the shelf behind the bar, inscribed with the words "Congratulations Kendra & Todd," must have caught her eye, because with one swift movement they were both smashed against the wall.

Kendra smiled with satisfaction as we stepped over the pile of shattered glass and headed out into the night.

14

The MGM Grand hotel is without a doubt the largest structure that I have ever been inside. Even when you are completely sober, it is a labyrinth of casinos, restaurants, and shops that seem to scroll along beside you in an endless loop. If you've already had a Long Island Iced Tea and a vodka shot you may as well just give yourself up for lost.

"Haven't you been to this club before?" I asked as we passed by lingerie clad blackjack dealers for the third time. That is one section of the casino you don't forget.

"Just a couple of times," she said. "And not once was I in my right mind." She veered me to the left, almost into a passing group of college guys who looked us up and down and whistled.

"Please tell me you guys are dentists," I said to them as we passed. One of them turned and walked backwards for a few steps.

"I'll be whatever you want me to be!" he yelled, arms outstretched.

"Aw, did you hear that?" I said to Kendra. "He'll be whatever I want him to be! Why couldn't you have run into *them* at Finnegan's?" I gave a few more glances and smiles over my shoulder before Kendra yanked me off to the right and we found ourselves at the entrance to the club. If we had only taken a left instead of a right when we had come in the main lobby we would have found it in about three minutes, rather than taking the grand tour. My heels were already starting to hurt.

Since we were half an hour too early to meet our man friends, and I was not willing to walk around a second longer to look for another bar to wait at, we paid our own cover charge and went into the club. We also reluctantly paid for our own first round of drinks and took a seat at a table, keeping an eye out for our dates as people slowly filtered in.

We had only been seated a few minutes when my phone began vibrating and Nick's name appeared on the screen. He'd been texting me all day, and he didn't quite sound like himself. Mostly he had been saying things about how he wished I had told him my feelings sooner, that maybe things would have been different between us. I didn't exactly know how to respond to that. I mean, was three years not enough time for him to figure out that I had feelings for him, and that maybe he felt the same way about me? All the opportunities he had over the years, did it really take a drunken text message, asking what he was wearing, for things to finally click?

Frankly, the more serious our texts and email became, the more Nick was starting to annoy me. I was starting to wish I had never initiated any of this flirtation, and after witnessing Kendra's meltdown tonight I was starting to feel a lot like the loathed Carlotta. I had become the other woman in my best friend's marriage.

I tried to cancel out the damage I had done by texting back neutral responses, and encouraging him to work things out with Megan instead of dwelling on what could have been. But he didn't seem to want to take the hint. I ignored his most recent text and was debating shutting off my phone entirely, when a message came through that wasn't from Nick. It was from Chris.

"Chris?" I said out loud.

"Brewer?" asked Kendra.

I looked up at her from the glow of my cell phone, regretting that I had said the name out loud. "Uh, yeah. I just got a text from him. I wonder what he wants?"

"You're such a little vixen," she said. "You've been here a month and already have the guys wrapped around your finger."

"Oh, please," I said. "It's not like that. This is *Chris* we're talking about. Last week I saw him drinking out of a Spiderman thermos bottle." I opened up his message, which was actually three messages:

2 girls found dead on the strip

Suspects r 2 middle-aged psycho dentists

If you know of their whereabouts call police ASAP

I laughed and was about to show it to Kendra when she started waving madly across the bar, as if the QE2 was leaving port.

"They're here!" she squealed, jumping out of her seat.

Striding towards us in a white linen button-up shirt and

dark jeans, was the one and only Bryce Storm. I recognized him from television the moment I saw him, and I must admit it was very exciting. I could practically smell the money wafting towards me from across the room as visions of a life of luxury flashed before my eyes. His hair was graying, but his face was tanned and unwrinkled, giving him that young-man-with-gray hair look that I have always kind of enjoyed.

My fantasy, however, came to a cymbal crashing halt when I tore my eyes away from Bryce and finally noticed the man standing by his side. The man with a million dollar smile and a penchant for one too many rum and Cokes. Tooth Model.

"Hey!" cooed Kendra, giving Bryce a full body hug. "Good to see you again! This is my friend Tessa." She motioned to me with her arm as if I were the next item up for bid on The Price is Right. The look on Tooth Model's face was priceless.

"Long time no see, huh?" I said. Tooth Model leaned in for a hug, which I gingerly returned. He still smelled like an alcoholic.

"You two know each other?" asked Kendra.

"We were seat mates on the plane," said Tooth Model. He eyed me up and down. "Can you believe it?"

I wondered if he remembered asking me to join the mile high club. I felt a little bit of my martini come back up into my mouth.

"No way!" said Kendra. "What a small world!"

"Super small," I mumbled. "So, Bryce was your famous dentist friend, huh?"

"I had a feeling you didn't believe me," said Tooth Model smugly. "Maybe now we can get to know each other a little better?" He turned the maraschino cherry he had in his mouth over with his tongue and flicked it out at me.

I turned to Kendra for help, but she was already swaying her hips to the music and running her hand up and down Bryce's arm. I knew it was only a matter of time before she pulled him onto the dance floor and left me to fend for myself. Not that I could blame her. I reminded myself that she was going through a tough time and that it was my job to be her wingman. If there was any chance of her sipping drinks at a swim-up bar in Jamaica with Bryce Storm, I needed to do my part to make it happen. That thought did not keep me from cringing when the next song to come on was the bikini car wash video we had been watching at the house.

"Oh my God! I love this song!" screamed Kendra in a high pitched drunk party-girl voice. She grabbed Bryce by the hand and dragged him onto the dance floor. The last thing I saw before they were swallowed up by the crowd was Kendra dipping down into the same ridiculous move she had tried in her basement.

"Ouch," I said out loud to myself. I couldn't hear the sound of her knee popping, but I knew it had happened. Tooth Model must have thought I was talking to him because the next thing I knew he had his hand out, motioning for me to join him on the dance floor.

"Ready to get your grind on?" he asked. I swear to God he said that. Am I ready to get my grind on. I laughed out loud in his face and grabbed my drink off the table.

"Sure," I said, not taking his hand. I walked towards the dance floor, letting him follow, and keeping any sort of hip sway to a bare minimum as I knew his eyes were plastered to my butt. I found a fairly roomy spot so we wouldn't need to get too close, and broke out the most asexual dance moves I could think of. I was about ten seconds away from doing the Running Man, when Tooth Model decided to turn on the low budget male stripper moves. I stood there watching in horror when a thought suddenly occurred to me. I reluctantly moved in a littler closer so he could hear me.

"Hey, how come you're still here?" I asked. "Wasn't the dental convention a few weeks ago?" He took the opportunity to put his slimy paw on my back.

"I flew back home!" he shouted, "And when I got there I found my clothes all over the front lawn. So I decided to come back to Vegas!"

"Why were your clothes all over the lawn?" I yelled.

"Because my wife's a bitch!" he yelled back.

"You're *married*?" Was there not a man on the planet who wasn't trying to cheat? I literally pried his fingers off of me and took a step backwards.

"Only on paper," he whispered, putting his lips practically inside my ear canal. I took two more steps backward, apologizing as I knocked into another couple. I shook my finger in Tooth Model's face and looked desperately in Kendra and Bryce's direction. They were caught up in a heavy duty make-out session and would not have noticed me if I rode through the club on a unicycle.

I spent the next two songs deflecting Tooth Model's advances and looking pleadingly at other guys on the dance floor, hoping that some other drunk would come rescue me. But nobody would bite. I couldn't blame them. If somebody were to ask the question "Who brought the weirdo?" I would need to raise my hand. I wouldn't want to dance with me either.

I felt my phone vibrating inside my purse and took the opportunity to excuse myself and head back to our table. I glanced over my shoulder to see that Tooth Model had already sidled up behind a new girl, who no doubt was getting a whiff of gin and the sudden urge to take a shower.

I looked at my phone, not even minding if it was Nick again. But it wasn't. It was Chris.

I heard if you don't start sucking face with the old dude you're fired.

Shocked, I glanced all around the bar, not seeing any familiar faces until I reached the far side of the dance floor, and there, standing alone by a post, was Chris. My hero. Powered by vodka and self-preservation, I ran towards him and threw my arms around his neck. I was so happy I could've kissed him. I didn't, but I could have.

"What are you doing here?" I asked. "You won't believe the creep Kendra set me up with! Well, I guess you would believe it, you just saw him for yourself."

"I overheard you two talking about your hot dates yesterday and I figured you may need some rescuing." His face had turned red when I hugged him. "I hope you don't think this is creepy, or that I'm like a stalker or something."

"Oh God no!" I said. "You could've been peeking in my hotel room windows tonight and still not be as creepy as that guy. I owe you big time." I had never seen Chris dressed so stylishly before. I took a step back and gave an exaggerated nod of approval to his powder blue button-up shirt and jeans.

He had even styled his hair.

"You look great!" I said.

"Thank you ma'am," said Chris, his face turning even redder.

"Let's go sit!" I grabbed his hand and led him to the bar where we could keep an eye on Kendra and Bryce who were currently still in a lip lock. Tooth Model was nowhere to be seen, which was fine by me.

Chris bought us a couple of drinks and we immediately had a fabulous time making fun of everybody on the dance floor - namely the sluts, the pervs, and the total douchebags. Chris and I were in our people-watching glory, and it was with a rush of glee that I glanced at the time and realized that the night was still young. I leaned in closer as we toasted each other with two tequila shots.

I had my hand resting on his knee when the latest Britney Spears song came on. And I was about to pull him onto the dance floor when Tooth Model suddenly materialized out of thin air. He sidled up with a smug "she's mine" look on his face, and tried to put his arm around me.

"Where have you been, babe?" he asked. "I've been looking all over for you."

I shrugged his arm off my shoulder and moved in closer to Chris.

"I forgot to tell you," I said. "I have a boyfriend. He just got back from Iraq! He came here right from the airport actually." Tooth Model took a step back and gave Chris the once over.

"This guy's your boyfriend?" he asked, flicking his finger

up and down.

I arched an angry eyebrow at Tooth Model, and then I did it - I kissed him. *Chris*, not Tooth Model. Please, don't make me sick. It was a mixture of wanting to piss off Tooth Model and being protective of this person who had gone out of his way to show up tonight in order to rescue me. So I leaned in and I kissed him. And he kissed me back. Then I put my hand on the back of his neck, and Chris put his hand around my waist, and I was no longer kissing him to get rid of Tooth Model, but I was kissing him because I liked it. By the time I looked up, Tooth Model was gone and Chris had turned as red as my BMW.

"Sorry." I shrugged, staring down at the floor. "I, uh, I just wanted to get rid of him."

When I looked back up, Chris had the same sheepish expression on his face that he gets every time he jams the photocopier.

"Actually, um, making out with me is one thing you never need to apologize for," he said. "I've kind of been wanting to do that ever since, well, ever since I met you."

My stomach did a swan dive off the Stratosphere and I smiled back at him. Had he always been this cute close up? I realized I still had my hand on the back of his neck. My finger twisted around a piece of his hair - hair that he had tousled up special for tonight, the night that he came to my rescue because he had been wanting to kiss me ever since I set foot in Las Vegas. I slid my hand from the back of his neck, down to his arm, and into his hand.

"Come on." I pulled him to his feet. "Dance with me." We disappeared onto the dance floor, happily pushed close by the crowd. He put his hand on my back and I leaned into his neck, the strobe lights turning everything into a slow motion dream. It was one of those dreams that leave you heartbroken when you awaken to find out that it wasn't real - but there was no chance of that tonight. Tonight it was me, Chris, and the dance floor, and everything, for the time being, was perfect.

***

It was nearly 1:00 a.m. before we saw Kendra and Bryce again. Chris and I were still on the dance floor when somebody grabbed me around the shoulders from behind. I had the horrible thought that it was Tooth Model coming back for more rejection, but it was only Kendra who looked much less perfectly done up than she had a few hours earlier. Her long blonde curls had frizzed up from the heat and sweat inside the club.

"Hey girl!" she screamed. Apparently Kendra was now using the phrase "hey girl." The look on her face when she noticed Chris standing there was that of a person seeing their dead grandfather rise up out of his coffin. "Oh my God! I'm so glad you're here!" She pulled him into an embrace and then tossed him off to the side. "I'm leaving with Bryce, he's got a suite upstairs," she whispered into my ear. I knew there had to be a reason she was so happy to see Chris, she felt guilty about ditching me.

"Are you sure?" I asked. "Don't do anything you'll regret." But seriously, who was I kidding? Nobody would regret sleeping with Bryce Storm. Bryce grabbed somewhere that I couldn't see, and Kendra started giggling like a mad woman as they headed for the exit.

"Chris will make sure I get home safe!" I shouted uselessly

at the back of their heads. "Kendra's got herself a rebound guy, huh?" asked Chris.

"One hell of a rebound," I said, watching his salt and pepper head, and the smell of money, disappear out the door. "You want to get out of here too?"

Chris and I chose to end our evening not in the fashion of Kendra and Bryce, but rather innocently with a walk down The Strip, just as far as my four inch heels would allow me. We walked for what seemed like miles, and laughed when we looked up and saw that we were still in front of the MGM Grand. I told you the place is enormous.

"That is one huge hotel," he said, staring up at it in awe. We were standing underneath the M.

"Yep," I said. Sometimes I have a way with words. Just then my phone started ringing from inside my purse and I pulled it out just to make sure it wasn't Kendra, though that was highly unlikely. This time it was Nick.

"Who's that?" asked Chris.

"Nobody," I said, and for the moment I meant it. I switched off the phone and put my arms around his neck.

"You know," he said, "I've lived here for years now. I hate the club scene, I never desired to go to the Bunny Ranch, and I never once wished to see Wayne Newton in concert. But ever since you came here," he leaned down and kissed me, "it kind of feels like home."

15

Shut up. Shut up! Oh dear God.

My phone was ringing and it needed to stop. I grabbed it off the nightstand and threw it across the room, then buried my face back into the pillows. The realization that I had a massive hangover became clearer the closer I came to consciousness, so fighting off consciousness was clearly the key to my survival. But my phone did not seem to agree, it just kept ringing. Whoever it was really *really* wanted to talk to me.

Thoughts of Kendra stranded on the side of the road drifted through my head, but they weren't enough to make me budge. I doubted Bryce Storm left women stranded on the sides of roads anyway. But what if it was Chris? I didn't want him to think there was any weirdness between us, so I heaved myself out of bed and turned on the lamp.

"Aw come on!" I yelled when it wasn't Chris's name that I saw on the screen. It was Kendra's, and it was only 8:40 a.m.

"Mmmmph," I answered.

"Hi!" she said, sounding awfully chipper and not at all like somebody stranded on the side of a road. I guess a night with Bryce Storm is enough to keep the hangover away. "Whatcha doing?"

"Shucking corn. What do you *think* I'm doing?" I headed into the bathroom just in case I threw up on the carpet. I enjoyed having a maid and everything, but I didn't really want to test the bounds of our relationship.

"Oh, yeah, I guess it is pretty early. Bryce got paged with an emergency and had to head out."

"Cosmetic dentists have emergencies?" I asked. I looked at myself in the mirror. My hair stood up in six directions and I had glitter on my neck. Had Chris been wearing glitter? I brushed it off with a tissue and sat down on the lid of the toilet.

"Sure they do. What do you think happens if an actor breaks a tooth and has to do a photo shoot? Anyway, that's not why I called. I thought we could go to the art museum today."

"Las Vegas has an art museum?" I asked.

"Las Vegas has a great art museum, we'll go check it out and annoy all the other people by gossiping loudly about our night, sound good?"

"Sure," I said. *This woman is fucking insane.* "Come get me in an hour." I flipped open the lid of the toilet, knelt down on the floor, and ended the conversation.

***

The car ride to the museum was mostly filled with Kendra talking about her night with Bryce in more detail than I ever needed to know. When her story about eating hot fudge sundaes in the Jacuzzi threatened to make its second appearance, I changed the subject to me and Chris. I told her about how Chris had come to my rescue, and how I'd kissed him only to get rid of Tooth Model but then didn't end up stopping until the wee hours of the morning. I told her that for the first time in three years Nick Trask wasn't the person I thought about as I drifted off to sleep. I half expected her to be shocked at my revelation, or to lecture me about the perils of office romance, but all she did was glance over at me and smile.

"You two work," she said with an approving nod. "I like it."

One fast food stop and one iced coffee later, we found ourselves wandering the halls of the Las Vegas Art Museum. The museum was larger than I had expected, and filled with mostly contemporary artwork. Several touristy looking women, who I imagined had lost their husbands to the casinos, were milling around. There were also a few parents with small children trying to force an appreciation for art on them that would need at least a few more years to develop, if ever. I hated art museums as a kid, and my parents brought me to them relentlessly. Perhaps subconsciously that is why I turned out to be an artist, but at the time they bored me to tears.

I smiled sympathetically at two kids sitting on a bench playing with a matchbox car that one of them had the foresight to smuggle in. With one exuberant push the little boy shot the matchbox car past his sister, off the end of the bench, and into the leg of an elderly woman. I laughed as their mother's threat of never taking them to a museum again was met with a joyful "Yes!" from both of the kids. I high-fived the little boy as he skipped out of the room.

"So I've always had this idea," said Kendra, as we strolled slowly from painting to painting, "there are all kinds of companies that cater to children, making pottery and building teddy bears and stuff. But why should they have all the fun?" She stopped in front of a painting of a man with no head who was playing darts. To the right of the painting was a blank canvas. To the right of the blank canvas was a third canvas depicting the dartboard with the headless man's head nailed to it by a dart.

"What on earth was this guy thinking?" asked Kendra, moving down the line. "Anyway, I always thought it would be cool to own my own business hosting art parties for adults. I could do bachelorette parties where everyone makes their own jewelry, or bridal showers, or even corporate events. Don't you think it would be fabulous if somebody came into Flamhauser-Geist with some supplies and taught us how to make something cool? It'd be a way better morale booster than those stupid trust falls Sharon made us do in the parking lot last year." I followed Kendra around as she spoke. She seemed so caught up in her speech that I wasn't even sure if she noticed I was still there.

"There are just so many people out there that would benefit from a little art in their lives, they're just never given the opportunity. I mean, I could even host events at nursing homes and hospitals, and give those people something to look forward to. We could do watercolors, or collages, or even - " She finally stopped walking and looked me in the eye. "Or even sculptures made out of paperclips. You know what I mean, Tessa?"

I actually did know. I knew a *lot.*

"That's not a bad idea," I said. I thought of my office supply sculptures and the enjoyment I got out of them. Perhaps Tom Skeeter had not enjoyed the time I spent building them when I should have been working, but they kept me sane and you can't argue with that.

"You know, Kendra, maybe we could do this. I mean, what are the odds that two artists would find each other the way we did? Maybe we're meant to kiss Flamhauser-Geist goodbye and just go for it!" Within two minutes I had latched onto the idea and for once saw myself becoming something more than an office drone. I saw myself happy and in my element. And then, at the sound of Kendra's laughter, I saw my bubble burst.

"Are you forgetting that I'm a Flamhauser?" she asked. "I hate to say it, but I'm in this for the long haul. I would need to publicly disgrace the entire company before my family ever let me off the engineering hook." She shook her head, some of the fire going out of her eyes. "It is a nice idea though. Maybe in another life."

"But that's not fair," I said. I wasn't letting this go so easily. "I mean, shouldn't you be doing what would make you happy? God, if I had the means to get out of this job I would in a second. No offense."

"None taken. But that's the thing, Tess. If I bail on the family company, I won't have the means either. Especially with Todd gone. You think my parents would support me if I decide to start dressing like a hippie and laying around in the grass painting rainbows?"

"Is that what you did in college?" I asked. I was having some trouble picturing Kendra dressed as a hippie, or even laying in grass.

"No," she said. "But that's the image my parents have of artists."

"Well that wouldn't be us," I said. "We would be businesswomen with clients, and a website, and some kind of van with our company logo on the side. There'd be no lounging around or smoking drugs, or whatever the heck your parents think artists do. And if we're a success, we wouldn't even need your parents help. Not for long."

"If we were successful, yes," said Kendra. "But what if we fail? We'd have no jobs, no money, and who knows if my family would even let me back into the business. We'd end up stripping at The Jiggly Kitty to make ends meet. And I for one do not want to give Rob Dorfman the satisfaction of seeing *that*."

"Okay," I said. "But if nobody ever took chances, then nothing would ever get accomplished would it? I mean, what if the guy who invented the Internet decided that it was too much of a risk?"

"Then we would never have known what we were missing out on, would we?" asked Kendra.

"That's a terrible attitude."

"Hey, don't think I haven't had this argument with myself plenty of times over the years," she said, raising her voice. I seemed to have struck a nerve. "It's just how it is. Luckily I actually do like being an engineer most of the time."

"You like building strip clubs?" I asked. "You like the fact that because of us some poor girl can now find a job as a stripper instead of at McDonald's? Or that because of us some guy with a wife and kids can travel less than ten minutes to the nearest Jiggly Kitty instead of going home to his family? Do you really like that? Because for me, it makes me feel kind of sick."

I should've just shut up, but I couldn't. I kept pushing the subject even though I could tell she was getting annoyed with me. "And how about the fact that it's your *dad* who started all of this, doesn't that gross you out at all? I mean he must make a lot of site visits."

Lack of sleep and residual drunkenness were certainly egging me on, but also, just maybe, a teensy bit of anger for ditching me with Tooth Model.

"Look," said Kendra, "if we didn't do it Rob would just find another engineering company that would. The stupid strip clubs would get built with or without us!"

We were standing face to face in the middle of the room, pretty much poised for a cat fight. The security guard by the door slowly inched his way toward us, either getting ready to break it up, or trying to get a front row seat.

"But it's all just so pointless," I said, tears starting to fill my eyes. "I'm twenty-eight years old, Ken, and what have I contributed to the world? Well-labeled file folders?" I sat down on a bench and hung my head in my hands. "I just don't want to do this anymore."

"I know," said Kendra, softening a bit. "But if you don't want to be a secretary anymore, then quit! If it's the money you're worried about. then keep your job and start something on the side. Sell your paper clip sculptures to one of the hotel gift shops, or put some up on eBay. Try *something*. But if you don't have the drive for it, don't turn it around and make it my fault. Don't make my unwillingness to be disowned by my entire family be your excuse for not even trying!"

Now she was the one who had struck a nerve. All the years I'd wasted behind a desk added up in my head and I suddenly felt like throwing up.

"Oh God." I stood up to run for the door, but it was too late. I threw up right there on the carpet, below the painting of the man throwing darts at his own head. The security guard beeped on his walkie talkie and called for a janitor. "Somebody just barfed in the Gardner Room," I heard him say. Lovely.

"Oh man," said Kendra coming over to rub my back. "Are you okay? I didn't think I upset you *that* much."

"I'm pretty sure it was the tequila shots, not you," I mumbled, wiping my mouth with my wrist. The last time I threw up in public I was nine years old and had just ridden the tea cups at Six Flags four times in a row. I apologized to the security guard on our way out.

"No problem, miss." He winked. "Nobody cares much for that painting."

16

I felt much better when I awoke for the second time that day. The air conditioning was cranked, and the home shopping channel that I had fallen asleep to was now selling a pair of awesomely awful looking pants. They had rhinestone pineapples all over them and came in horrific colors like watermelon and lime green. I sat up in bed and marveled as the counter showing how many people were currently purchasing the awful pants continued to climb. I can, and have, watched the home shopping channel for hours. I find it oddly comforting, and it warmed my soul when Gertrude from Alabama called in to say that she had just purchased a pair for her daughter-in-law.

I got out of bed and headed into the bathroom for a quick shower, thanking the Lord the entire way that I did not yet have a mother-in-law. I needed to spruce myself up since Chris had called right after I got back from turning the Las Vegas Art Museum into a vomitorium. I invited him over once I was able to sleep off the worst of my hangover.

I drowned myself in coconut body wash and changed into a pink Jiggly Kitty sweatshirt. Then I brushed my teeth about forty-seven times. A cloud of coordinating coconut body spray was my final attempt to cover the alcohol still radiating from my pores. In all honesty, I was a bit nervous about seeing him. Not nervous in a bad way, but more like I was unsure how to act. I mean, was he expecting another make-out session? Did he think I had invited him over for a little afternoon delight? Or were we just going to hang out and watch television like nothing had happened?

In the short time we had known each other, there had never been any awkwardness between Chris and I, and I hoped that this new development would not change things for the worse. I really wanted us to both be on the same page, whatever page that may be.

The late afternoon sun was pouring in when Chris finally knocked on my door. He had a backpack on one shoulder and a Monopoly board tucked under his arm. In his hand was a giant bottle of red Gatorade, exactly what I had been craving ever since I woke up.

"You are the absolute best coworker ever," I said, taking a huge gulp from the bottle before he could even come in the door. "I feel like I've been sucking on sweat socks. How are you holding up?"

"I was pretty dead this morning, I'll admit. But then I remembered that I wasn't the one who defiled a fine art museum and I felt a whole lot better."

I punched him in the arm as he brushed past me into my room. He was wearing another button-up shirt, but this time with a Metallica concert t-shirt underneath.

"Very funny," I said. "So what's with the backpack? You going camping after you leave here?"

"I just brought some entertainment for us." He surveyed my suite with an approving nod. "Nice place, geez. One time the company sent me to Albuquerque and put me up in a Motel 6."

"The difference is that you weren't traveling with Kendra," I said, closing the door behind him. It had been strange enough seeing Chris in the club last night, but it was even stranger seeing him here in my hotel room with my clothes and makeup all over the place. I felt like I was giving away some sort of secret. I quickly ducked into the bathroom after the thought that maybe I had left a box of tampons on the sink refused to leave my head. But it was all clear, and I started to breathe a little easier.

I watched as he dumped the contents of his backpack out on my bed. Besides Monopoly, he had brought travel sized versions of Scrabble and Battleship, plus an assortment of DVD's. I smiled when I saw them because this was not a guy who had come over expecting action. This was just Chris being good old nerdy Chris.

"Board games are lame, I know," he said, misinterpreting my smile. "But with the right company, they can be fun." He gave me a wink and told me to take my pick. I immediately went for Monopoly - my reasoning being that it would take the longest to play, and I really didn't want him to leave. We set up on the coffee table in the living area and I put the home shopping channel on the television, just for "background noise," though Chris didn't believe me for a second. The next item up was a tote bag bejeweled with creatures from the sea.

"Are those lobsters?" I asked. It was hard to tell exactly, there were so many rhinestones.

"It's definitely some kind of mollusk," said Chris.

"What the heck is a mollusk anyway?"

"I'm not sure, let's find out." Chris fished around in his backpack and pulled out a dictionary.

"Oh my God, you are such a loser." I laughed. "You're carrying a dictionary around in there?"

"Hey it's for Scrabble, okay?" He flipped through the pages. "Here we go, mollusk, an invertebrate having a calcareous shell of one, two, or more pieces that wholly or partly enclose the soft, unsegmented body, and live in aquatic or damp habitats."

"Yes, that sounds exactly like something I'd want on my handbag," I said.

"Oh come on, Tess. I know you ordered one in every color before I got here."

"I swear to you, I am in love with this channel but I've never ordered anything!" That wasn't entirely true, but what Chris didn't know wouldn't hurt him. As I counted out $1,500 in play money to each of us, I glanced at my closet to make sure the door was shut. "Here, you and your dictionary can be the top hat. Sir Dorkus McDorkington, I presume." I tossed it in his direction.

"Thanks, that's sweet of you."

We played happily for the next few hours. The sun went down and the lamps came on. Coffee was made and pizza was ordered. Embarrassing stories from high school were exchanged. I found out that Chris had played trombone in the marching band. Chris found out that I had once dug through a bag of cafeteria garbage to find my retainer. The home shopping channel, when Chris couldn't stand it anymore, was switched over to TV Land for old episodes of Leave it to Beaver.

I have never in my life met another person who wanted to watch that show with me. I mean, even my parents seem to find it boring. But here, in the City of Sin, I found someone. Despite the fact that I was losing horribly at Monopoly, I hadn't had such an enjoyable afternoon in a very long time.

Chris had built up a rather impressive empire of hotels along one side of the board, and on my next roll I landed on Boardwalk. I looked down at my pile of ones and fives, and then over at my properties which were almost all mortgaged.

"Seems I'm out of money," I said, devilishly curling my ponytail around my finger. "Do you accept any other forms of payment?"

"Well, I can take a check, but it would need the approval of Mr. Pennybags," said Chris. "I haven't seen him around though, have you?"

"No, Mr. Pennybags isn't here." I slid a little closer to him on the floor. "Any other ideas?"

"Maybe," he said. I slid a little closer still, and looked up into his face.

"Hi."

"Hi."

He leaned in close, and oh my, whatever cologne he was wearing smelled absolutely delicious. Or maybe that was just what Chris smelled like without any help at all. Maybe it was just a really long time since I'd had myself a boyfriend. Whatever it was, kissing Chris sober was just as good as kissing him drunk, maybe even more so since we both had gotten in a bit of practice.

I ran my hand inside his shirt and down his arm, feeling the muscles he had been hiding from the world, or at least from his coworkers. I pushed him down onto his back, right there in front of the television.

"Do you think it's weird to make-out in front of a 1950's sitcom?" I asked, after a while. "The Beav's going to have to learn about this stuff sooner or later," he said. He flipped me over and played with the zipper of my sweatshirt. "You are one beautiful secretary, you know that?" I felt myself blush and I turned to look at the television instead of Chris.

"I'm really glad you came over," I said, watching Wally try to explain why there was an alligator in the bathtub. "I like you."

"You like me, or you *like* like me?"

"Let's just say that if you were still playing the trombone, and I was still searching through chicken patties for my retainer, I would definitely have one of my friends ask you out for me."

"Ah, so you *like* like me."

"Seems that way."

We laid there on the floor for a while longer, my head on Chris's chest, lamenting the fact that tomorrow was Monday and the start of another work week.

"We should probably finish the game," Chris said at last. "It's getting late."

I sat up and looked from the game board, to my pathetic

pile of cash, then back to the board. "I think the game's pretty much finished, remember? That's how we got started corrupting the Beaver."

"Oh yeah."

We cleaned up the game and the food, and then Chris put his backpack on his shoulder. I suddenly felt extremely lonely, even though he was still standing right there.

"Let's call in sick tomorrow," I begged. "We can play Battleship."

Chris pushed me up against the door and gave me quite a passionate kiss goodbye, then he looked into my eyes. I thought he was about to tell me that he loved me, I swear I did. I held my breath.

"Can't," he said. "Rob needs a concept plan drawn up by noon."

Ah yes, nothing like the mention of Rob Dorfman to kill a mood.

"That was *not* romantic," I said, and pushed him out of my room. I leaned out the door and smiled as I watched him walk toward the elevators. He blew me an exaggerated kiss before getting on, and I caught it in an equally dorky fashion.

I shut the door and slid down to the carpet, my stomach in knots. It was, by far, the best I'd felt all day.

***

Not ten minutes had passed when there was a knock at the door. My heart beat a bit faster at the idea that it was Chris, unable to wait until tomorrow to see me again. I flung open the door and stopped short of throwing myself into his arms.

Good thing I didn't, because it wasn't Chris at all.

There, in my doorway, stood Nick Trask.

17

"Hi," said Nick, standing in my doorway completely unannounced. Completely unannounced, standing in my doorway, in Las Vegas. Three thousand miles out of context. I was having a hard time wrapping my hung over brain around what was going on. But before I could even attempt to think, he was pulling me into a giant bear hug and spinning me around in the air.

"Wha-what are you doing here?" I stuttered as he plunked me back down on the ground. I looked from Nick's brown puppy dog eyes, which were staring into mine, to the suitcase on the floor next to him. "Wha-what's that?" I pointed dumbly at the suitcase. I couldn't stop stuttering.

"Is this a bad time?" he asked. He was totally casual, as if it were the most normal thing in the world for him to be here right now. He looked me up and down and I realized I must have been a little disheveled, as if I were just rolling around on the floor with a guy.

"Uh, no," I said, zipping my sweatshirt practically up to my chin. "I was just about to get ready for bed. Come on in." I stepped aside and checked him out as he walked into my room. Even after getting off a six hour flight, he still looked like an Abercrombie & Fitch model. But that didn't matter right now. Nothing mattered except for what the hell he was doing here, and why hadn't he at least called?

"I tried calling you last night," he said, reading my mind. "But you never picked up."

Oh yes, now I remembered. Standing under the M with Chris, my phone ringing, and me shutting it off. Things had melted into a pleasant haze after that point and I honestly hadn't given Nick a second thought since.

"Oh, that's right. I was out with my boss. I couldn't really hear my phone in the clubs." I glanced all over my room for evidence that Chris had just been there. Not that it mattered, as I had every right to have a guy in my room. Nick was the one who was married, not me.

I followed him over to the couch where he dropped his bags on the floor and flopped himself down. He put his feet up on the coffee table where Chris and I had just played Monopoly.

"Um, Nick," I said. "Really, you know I'm thrilled to see you, as always. But can I just ask you something that's been on my mind since you walked in here about thirty seconds ago?"

"Shoot."

"Okay, well, don't take this the wrong way, but what the hell are you doing here?"

"You don't *seem* very thrilled to see me, Tessa," he said, ignoring my question. "I'm a little disappointed." He stretched his arms along the back of the couch and yawned.

"No, of course I am." I sat down on the couch next to him trying to ignore the tanned arm behind my head, the one that was threatening to tear right through his t-shirt. And also, oh dear, that cologne. Why did men have to keep coming into my room smelling so delicious? "It's just that I don't really understand why you're here."

Nick pulled his cell phone out of his jeans and flipped it open. He kept glancing up at me and smiling as he scrolled through something.

"I had a dream last night that you and I - " Nick had started reading one of the text messages I sent him out loud.

"Oh God, please stop!" I cut him off and pressed my face into my hands.

Suddenly Nick's hand was on the back of my head, stroking my hair.

"Hey, you asked," he said.

"Please, please, tell me that there's another reason," I begged, peeking up at him from behind my fingers.

Nick stared at me for a few seconds, and then I felt his hand fall from the back of my head.

"Alright, well, there is a tiny bit more to it. I was getting ready to go home on Friday, when Marvin stopped by my office," said Nick. Marvin was Marvin Frackman, Nick's boss. "He was all fired up about this guy Jimmy Cannon who's in town. He owns some grocery stores, but he's also started opening up strip clubs that compete with Dorfman's. Loose Cannons they're called, ever heard of it?"

I shook my head.

"Anyway, Marvin found out where Jimmy was having dinner, and he wanted me to tagalong to try to drum up some business." Nick stood up and helped himself to a beer from my fridge, as if he'd lived here for months. "I tried to tell him that I couldn't go, that Meg would kill me if I got home late one more time, but he wouldn't take no for an answer."

"And so you went?" I asked.

"If I help get a new client, my status in this company will skyrocket. I'd be kind of like...like you." He smiled as he motioned to my rock star-like display of alcohol.

"Right," I said. "Kendra just went a little overboard. Trust me, my status hasn't gone anywhere." I settled back into the pillows, relaxing a bit. "But I thought you didn't want to become like those guys in upper management?"

"Hey, money talks." Nick shrugged. "Although, more status means more stress. And more fights with the wife."

"Speaking of whom," I looked expectantly at Nick, "where is the wife?"

"Well, Marv and I ended up stalking Jimmy all over Boston until eleven o'clock. By the time I got home it was after midnight and Megan had already packed her bags and went to stay with her parents. I didn't know what to do. She wouldn't take any of my calls, then *you* wouldn't take any of my calls. I just needed to see you." He paused and sat down on the couch facing me. For the second time in one day I felt as if a guy were about to confess his love.

"I needed to find out if maybe I made a mistake," he said.

"What, what, kind of mistake?" I immediately tensed up again.

"I'm wondering if maybe I married the wrong girl." He stared into my eyes as he spoke those words, and then he picked up my hand and held it against his cheek. After all these years, everything I'd ever dreamed about was actually happening. Yet here I was, ready to smother Nick with a pillow before I'd let it continue. I jumped up and walked over to the window, anything to get out of his line of vision.

"But you did marry Megan. You love Megan. And *this,*" I motioned back and forth to the two of us, "is not doing anything to help." I suddenly got a very clear picture of Megan in my head. She had just found out where her husband had disappeared to and was at this very minute boarding a plane to Vegas in order to shoot me in the head. It was time to panic.

"Shit, Nick, you need to get out of here!" I grabbed him by the hands and tried to pull him up from the couch, but he weighed about a billion pounds and I couldn't move him. He just kept looking at me like I was nuts.

"I can't go back *now,*" he said. "It's too late."

"Planes fly all night long! There's probably ten of them just sitting there on the runway, they'd love to have you!"

"Don't be silly, Tessa. Just let me stay the night. Megan couldn't care less, she's the one who left *me*, remember?" I was still holding onto his hands and he pulled me forward so I was about three inches from his face.

"What are you doing?" I asked in horror.

"What do you think?" He stood up and put his arms around my waist. "I've been going crazy thinking about all those texts, haven't you?"

He leaned in and kissed me, and suddenly any thoughts I

had of Megan coming to murder me just faded into the background. As did, and I'm ashamed to admit it, any thoughts I was having about Chris. Because Nick, *my* Nick, was kissing me at last. Okay so we hadn't just spent the day bonding over a game of Monopoly, and maybe Nick hadn't come to my rescue when I'd needed him most. But for that moment, all I knew was that I was making out with the love of my life. The love of my life, who also happened to be my closest friend in the world. Well, at least until I had met...until I had met....what the heck was his name? Chris. Yes, Chris. I tried to focus, really I did. But this was Nick for Christ sake. My mind had left the rest of my body to its own devices several minutes ago. Nick sat back down on the couch and pulled me onto his lap, when suddenly it hit me.

"You don't just taste like beer," I said, pulling away.

"I had a few cocktails on the plane," said Nick. He shrugged and pulled me back towards him.

"Oh God, no!" My stomach turned at the thought of hard liquor. I scrambled off of his lap and ran for the bathroom.

"Good to see you too!" yelled Nick as I slammed the door and threw up for the third time in one day.

18

On Monday morning Kendra was in full boss mode. I had a feeling that she was still angry with me after our argument in the museum because she had a whole list of tasks prepared, none of which involved my being around the office. It was just as well. I was a little concerned that Nick might show up at the office with a bouquet of roses or something, and I was not exactly planning to tell Chris about my new roommate.

Nick had slept on the couch and I had used my hangover as an excuse to avoid any further make-out sessions. Once I was in bed and able to think clearly again, that's when the guilt really took over, and it was coming at me from all sides. Chris sent me a few texts about how much fun he'd had with me that day, and I replied from underneath the blankets as if I needed to hide what I was doing from Nick. I told Chris that I felt the same way. And it was true. Everything I said to him was true, with the one minor omission that I had just made out with another guy who, by the way, was also sleeping in my living room.

Who on Earth was I turning into? This needed to stop. I just needed to figure out the right way to tell Nick that my flirting had been a mistake. Once I got that out of the way, and Nick went home to Megan, I could finally be with Chris guilt-free. I mean, how long could Nick possibly stay in Vegas anyway? Flamhauser-Geist isn't exactly generous with their vacation time.

I grabbed Kendra's list of tasks and headed outside to my BMW. I still gasp a little bit every time I get into the car, and then I usually take a few minutes to admire my tanned self in the rear view mirror. Yes, I know, it's materialistic and superficial, but for the time being this life and all its ridiculous accessories are *mine,* and I have a right to enjoy them. I turned up the radio and leaned my head back, soaking up the sun before starting the engine. *If you're mad at me, Kendra, you could've come up with a much worse punishment than sending me out of the office.*

I peeled out of the parking lot and headed toward my first stop which was to pickup Kendra's dry cleaning. You can't get much more stereotypically administrative assistant than picking up dry cleaning. I didn't really mind though because the dry cleaner was right next door to my favorite coffee shop, and I stopped in for a cappuccino. I took a seat on the patio rather than returning to my car. It was only 9:00 a.m. and Kendra's list wasn't all that long anyway.

As I sipped my coffee, my thoughts drifted to Kara who I had only spoken to twice on the phone since coming to Vegas. I felt a pang of guilt as I thought of all the time I had been spending with Kendra. I took out my cell phone to give her a call, and also give her a reason to leave the office for a few minutes. She would probably go out on the back steps that overlooked the parking lot where her car was parked between two empty spaces - one for my car, and one for Nick's. She was probably lonely. Neither one of us has many other girlfriends. Suddenly I couldn't dial the numbers fast enough. It rang six times before the familiar voice picked up.

"Good morning, Flamhauser-Geist, this is Kara."

"Okay, first of all," I said, "I am a horrible, horrible friend because I just realized how few times I've talked to you since I came out here. So feel free to trash my cubicle."

"Already trashed it last night," she said. "You're not a horrible friend though, you're just busy. I actually stopped calling you since that time your psycho boss grabbed the phone and started screaming Love Shack at me, remember?"

I laughed. Kendra and I had been at a karaoke bar when she got her paws on my cell. "Sorry about that, she's got a few issues to work out."

"I would start with singing lessons," said Kara. "Then maybe move on to rehab. Hey let me go outside before I get busted for taking personal calls at my desk. Hang on." I mentally followed her through the office, past each desk, and out the back door. Just as my imaginary Kara arrived on the back steps, the real one came back on the line.

"Okay, I'm out. So what's up?"

"Well, for starters, Nick's not in today is he?" I figured if she had known he was coming to Vegas she would have at least put in a courtesy call to fill me in. At least I hoped she would have.

"Uh, no, he's not. How'd you know that?"

"Because he's asleep in my hotel room." There was silence on the other end. Then I heard what sounded like muffled swear words. "Are you there?"

"Yeah, I'm here," said Kara. "Shit, Tessa, I'm sorry. I would've told you sooner, but I never thought he'd do anything this drastic."

"Told me what? What did he say? I need to know, Kara. I did something I shouldn't have and now things are getting out of hand."

"Um, he kind of told me on Friday that he thinks he's in love with you," said Kara.

"What?!"

"He said he never realized it while you were here, but now that you're away he hasn't been able to stop thinking about you."

"Oh God, what have I done?" I drummed my fingers on the table.

"He also said something about how he never thought you had feelings for him until a couple of weeks ago? Something to do with text messages. I don't know Tessa, we were out at a bar and it was loud and stuff. I couldn't really get all the details.

"That's okay," I said. "I know what he's referring - "

I suddenly stopped tapping my fingers. A pigeon on the opposite end of my table looked up at me expectantly, mid-peck. "Wait, when were you out at a bar with Nick?"

"Friday," she said. "After work."

"This Friday?"

"Yes, this Friday, as in three days ago. Megan was at her sister's bachelorette party and he didn't want to go home."

He lied to me.

"So he never went out with Marvin to network with some guy from Loose Cannons?" I asked. I was slowly getting a migraine.

"No way," she said. "He was with me all night. Well, not *all* night, but you know what I mean. Besides, we got the Loose Cannons account weeks ago. I guess Marvin and Tom stalked the guy all over Boston, which is a little creepy if you ask me."

I couldn't believe it. Megan was probably at home worried sick. Meanwhile, Nick is in Las Vegas borrowing stories from other people's lives in order to manipulate his best friend. The same best friend he spent the last three years taking for granted until she sent him a few dirty texts. I took three Advil out of my purse and swallowed them with my coffee.

"I thought you had a crush on him?" asked Kara. "Why are you so upset about all this anyway?"

"I do, I mean, I did," I said. "It's just that I met somebody else. Somebody who probably wouldn't have married a girl from a cruise ship after he'd met me."

"Is it serious?" asked Kara.

"It could be." I smiled to myself. "But I've made such a mess. Why couldn't I leave things alone with Nick? Things happen for a reason, don't they? I should've known when he married Megan that him and I just weren't meant to be."

"True," said Kara. "But if things happen for a reason, then so did this. Maybe it happened this way so you'd finally be able to let him go."

The pigeon cocked its head at me, waiting for my reply.

Kara had a point.

"You are so wise for a receptionist," I said. "So what do you think I should do?"

"You've got to send him back home. You've got to tell him that it's too late."

I sighed as I pictured all my artwork lined up along Nick's windowsill. He had been an awesome friend to me all these years, and it was highly unlikely that things could go back to normal between us. I imagined passing him in the hall and pretending to check my watch in order to avoid eye contact. But it was me who had started this whole mess. Me and whoever invented text messaging, the stupid idiot. I needed to accept the consequences.

Besides, when I thought of all the lies Nick had told me and the kind of man he was turning out to be, my idealistic opinion of him began to shift. Maybe he wasn't the awesomest friend on the planet after all. Maybe he was a jerk.

I gulped down the last of my coffee and said goodbye to Kara. I promised to let her know as soon as I had shipped Nick back to Massachusetts.

I pulled into the next place on Kendra's list and looked up at the sign. *Mocha Fresco* it said in large brown letters, except in place of the "o" in "Fresco" there was a coffee cup with a paintbrush poised above it. Kendra hadn't really given me any instructions on what to do at this place, just that I should give her name to the girl at the counter. I went inside and waited by the register for somebody to help me. It seemed to be some kind of art gallery/coffee shop combo. I liked it.

A girl with a neon pink pixie cut finally appeared out of a

back room and smiled cheerfully at me. "Can I help you?" she asked.

"Yes," I said. "Kendra Stoltz asked me to stop by here. She didn't really tell me why though, so I was kind of hoping you knew?"

"Ah," said the girl. "You must be Tessa?"

"Uh, yeah, that's me." *Why would she know my name?*

"Just a sec." She winked at me before ducking below the counter. I heard her shuffling through some papers.

"My name's Holly," she said when she finally popped back up. "If you'll just sign this form I can give you a little tour of the place. You're not actually scheduled until Wednesday, but I can show you around."

"Scheduled for what?" I asked. "I thought I was just supposed to pick up something for my boss?"

"Well, if your boss is Kendra Stoltz, she called here this weekend and rented out studio space in your name. Twice a week, starting this Wednesday and continuing for an 'undetermined amount of time.' She asked that it be stocked with some strange supplies." She pulled out another paper and began reading from it "Paper towel rolls, coffee filters, stirrers, bottle caps, and, I quote, 'any other materials that would normally be thrown in the garbage.'" She glanced up at me. "Are you some kind of trash collector?"

"I guess you could call me that," I laughed.

Holly shrugged. "Hey, we get all kinds here. There's a guy who comes in on Mondays with a trash bag full of dog hair. Come on, I'll give you a tour."

Studio space! All for me! I couldn't believe it. I followed Holly around the studio, smiling at the other people who were there, peacefully working on different projects. The main part of the shop was set up with tables for workshops, and off to the side was the coffee bar, some comfortable looking couches, and a fireplace. Artwork for sale by local artists lined the walls. Through a door in the back were the three private studios, each with their own skylights, and shelves stocked with everything I could possibly need.

"You look excited," said Holly. "You've got a very generous boss."

"You have no idea!" I said.

Here I was, thinking that Kendra was mad at me, when she had really been doing something like *this*. I practically skipped through the parking lot to get to my car. Wednesday was two whole days away and I was already itching to get my hands on some materials besides paperclips and pushpins. I would finally be an artist again, without anybody from HR ratting me out for stealing office supplies.

19

I called Nick as soon as I got in the car. Between my conversation with Kara and the excitement of finding out I had my own studio, I was pretty fired up and ready to tell him exactly what I thought about everything he had done.

"Hey you," answered Nick, on the fourth ring.

Oh God, I'm now a "you." This is even worse than I thought.

"What are you doing?" I asked. The sound of buildings and cars being blown up echoed in the background.

"Pay-per-view. I hope you don't mind. You're not paying for this stuff anyway, right?"

"Uh, yeah," I said. "Just keep it clean." Thoughts of Margaret Sherman reviewing an itemized list of dirty pay-per-view movies gave me the cold sweats. "Look, I'll meet you in the restaurant downstairs in fifteen minutes, ok? We need to talk." I hung up without waiting for a response and turned onto Las Vegas Boulevard.

I had gotten used to driving up and down The Strip. By now it was an every day occurrence to pull up alongside beautiful people in beautiful cars - and after a month of hanging out with Kendra, I had almost become a beautiful person myself. I stopped at a traffic light outside The Mirage and eyed my oversized sunglasses and diamond studded hoop earrings in the mirror - fake diamonds, of course, as I am still existing on an admin's salary.

But if you didn't know any better, you might think that I've lived here all my life. Two cute guys in a Mercedes tooted their horn as they passed me and turned into the hotel. Tourists. Or maybe members of a soon-to-be bachelor party. Whatever they were here for, they had come to escape the real world. And here I am, fortunate enough for my real world to have ended up in Las Vegas.

Over the past few days I've actually been toying with the idea of staying in Vegas permanently. I mean sure, I would have the same lousy secretarial job no matter where I moved. But at least here there is sunshine year round, and bright lights, and excitement. There's a really great guy named Chris. What's waiting for me back home? My family, yes. But there are planes and cell phones and the Internet, so staying connected isn't really an issue these days. Besides, it's *my* life we're talking about, and my family would want me to be happy, right? And sure, I might miss the changing of the seasons and all the hoopla over pumpkins and foliage and chirping birds. But in all honesty, the birds do start to get on your nerves after a while.

And yes, I understand that if I were to stay in Las Vegas I wouldn't have the hotel suite, or the BMW, or the expense account, forever. I would, however, have the chance to look back at my life and say that I did something kind of awesome. Something that didn't involve filing, or ordering sandwiches, or

Rob Dorfman. But really, I was just kicking the idea around.

I pulled into the Marriott and parked the car, pushing my sunglasses to the top of my head as I walked toward the entrance. I felt as if I was being watched. I scanned the windows of the restaurant and sure enough, there was Nick already seated at a table and drinking a beer. He didn't take his eyes off of me as I walked. Had he really told Kara that he was in love with me? I felt a flutter in my stomach as I remembered all the times he had hugged me goodnight after a night out after work, and all the nights I had cried myself to sleep after he had gotten married. I thought about all of the flirting that had led up to this very moment. We had just been joking around, hadn't we?

But then Nick left his wife and snuck off to Vegas, and, in the most tragic case of bad timing ever, decided that he wanted to be with *me*. Maybe a month ago I would have been game for whatever this entailed, but I was a changed woman now. I had higher standards and self respect. But Nick hadn't changed. Oh no. Nick looked the same and he probably smelled the same. That famous crooked smile he was giving me as I walked towards his table was definitely the same. His hair looked as if he had been surfing all day, even though I knew he had only been lounging around in my hotel room, the lazy bastard. Maybe he had been lounging around in my bed. My heart beat a little faster.

You're a fickle, spineless idiot, Tessa Golden.

I told the voice in my head to shut up as I sat down at the table. Nick had already ordered me a glass of wine and we locked eyes as he handed it to me. My old friend, the one who had gotten me through many a bad day, and who had my artwork lined up along his windowsill, had finally come for me.

The one thing that home had that Vegas didn't, was Nick. And right then, despite all my rationalizations, I knew I was a goner.

***

With a glass of wine rushing to my head, I tried to tell Nick that he needed to go home. I told him that I was mad at him for lying to me and that he was messing everything up by being here. I told him that the things I said in those text messages had been a mistake. But everything that I said just sounded like a joke. My words were weak and unconvincing, and so he went right ahead and ordered me another glass. The next thing I knew, we were taking the elevator back up to my suite, and then we were over by my bed, and then Nick was running his hands through my hair the way I always imagined he would.

In my mind this moment was years in the making and I looked into his eyes waiting for him to tell me that he too had been longing for it ever since the day we'd met. But Nick didn't speak. Instead he just unbuttoned my shirt. I decided to take the initiative and whispered something similar into his ear. I paused to allow him to say the same in return, but he still didn't say a word. Instead he slipped my shirt down over my shoulders. I wanted desperately for him to say that seeing me each day at the office was torture, or that he was sorry for having made me wait all these years. But he didn't say any of those things, and with each passing minute my fantasy of what this moment would be like started to collapse in on itself.

That's when I noticed the red plastic Monopoly hotel laying under the nightstand and the sight of it brought everything to a screeching halt. My cell phone started ringing from across the room and I pushed Nick away as I ran to get it. He pulled me back and told me to ignore it.

"I can't ignore it!" I protested. "It's probably Kendra. It could be important."

"More important than this?" Nick grabbed my hand and ran it down -

"No, Nick, stop it! This isn't right. I have to get the phone." I wrenched my arm out of his grip and grabbed the phone from my purse. It *was* Kendra.

"Hey, what's up?" I said, breathless.

"Tessa, oh thank God. I need you to get back here right away." She sounded frantic, almost as if she had been crying. "The filing deadline for Reno is tomorrow! *Tomorrow* Tessa! How could I have forgotten this?"

Actually, Kendra had been forgetting a lot of things lately - deadlines, meetings, personal hygiene. I am not saying that she stopped showering or anything, but she was losing her ability to look great no matter what had happened the night before. Sometimes her hair looked as if she hadn't bothered to comb it, and one day she came into the office wearing sweats. Not even stylish sweats, just plain old Hanes. And from time to time, I noticed the smell of alcohol on her, even if we hadn't gone out together the night before.

"Calm down, Ken. I'll be right there and we'll figure it out together, ok?" I scurried around the room collecting my items of clothing as I spoke.

"Ok," she squeaked, and hung up.

"I'm sorry, Nick. I have to get back to work. There's a Jiggly Kitty crisis going down." I pulled my shirt back on and buttoned it up with shaking hands.

"So you're just going to leave me here like this?" asked

Nick. He zipped up and leaned back on the bed on his elbows.

"This was a bad idea, I don't even know what I was thinking." I was suddenly very angry at myself for what I'd almost let happen. "Look, if you're going to stay here, you should probably get your own room. Flamhauser isn't going to be happy if they find out I have a houseguest."

Sure Tessa, blame it on the company. Don't tell him that it's you who doesn't want him here. You wouldn't want to hurt the adulterer's feelings. I told the voice in my head that I didn't have time for its crap right now, and drove a little crazily through the streets of Las Vegas.

I raced into work and felt a twinge of guilt when I passed by Chris and Dan's office. There was Chris, sitting innocently at his desk, none the wiser to what I had almost done. At the sound of my footsteps he turned his head and glanced over his shoulder. I smiled, but he seemed to look right through me and then turned back to his computer. I turned around to see if maybe somebody else was behind me - somebody Chris didn't want to talk to, like Roberta - but it was just me.

I shook off the slight pit that was forming in my stomach and continued into Kendra's office. There she was on the floor, surrounded by paperwork and plans, her hair in a messy pile on the top of her head fastened by a plastic clip I haven't seen the likes of since 1987. Her appearance had deteriorated since I'd seen her that morning. She looked up at me with red, mascara-smudged, eyes - a classic nutcase.

"Thank God you're here," she said. "I don't know if I can get this done by tomorrow morning. I really messed up this time."

I sat down on the floor next to her and looked around.

There were all kinds of redlined applications, zoning rules & regulations with sticky notes on them, and several empty cups of coffee. "Don't worry, we'll get this done. I'm not going anywhere until we do," I said. "But first, I need to thank you for Mocha Fresco. Nobody's ever done anything that nice for me before."

Kendra just shook her head and shrugged. "You deserve a chance to get out of here. Just because my life turned out to be shit, doesn't mean yours has to." She stabbed at one of the applications with her red pen. "There's still hope for you."

"There's hope for both of us," I said. "You don't have to self-destruct just because you hit a few bumps." I collected a few empty coffee cups off the floor and placed them in the trash. "Look, Ken, I think maybe we should take it easy with the drinking. I mean, what will Tom say if he finds out you had to join AA after spending three months with me?"

I meant it as a joke, but I didn't get any reaction. Kendra simply handed me some applications and told me that if I really wanted to help her I would start typing. Of course, when hasn't typing meaningless drivel about parking space dimensions and maximum pole heights solved all the problems of the world? I headed sullenly back to my office, resolving to pick the issue up again at a better time, when I ran smack into Chris. We literally collided in the hallway and yet he still managed to ignore me. This time it was too much. I chased him for a few steps and put my hand on his arm until he turned around and looked at me.

"What the heck's wrong with you?" I asked.

"Nothing," he said.

"Nothing?"

"Yeah, I'm just busy."

"Too busy to even say 'excuse me' when you just ran over me back there?" I asked. "Come on, what's wrong?"

"Fine." Chris rolled his eyes. "Tell me who the guy is."

My heart stopped. "What are you talking about?"

"You know what I'm talking about," he said. "I stopped by your hotel during lunch to leave something for you at the front desk."

"You did?" I squeaked.

"Yeah. I'm not surprised you didn't see me though, you seemed pretty occupied with that guy. Holding hands...drinking wine...that was quite the errand Kendra must've sent you out on."

"Oh, that guy," I said lamely, running my hand through my hair. I wasn't prepared for this. "He's just a friend from home, he uh, he flew in unexpectedly. We were just having lunch." *Sure Tessa, that's it. The 3,000 miles cross-country lunch date. Who wouldn't buy that?*

"Right," said Chris. "Strange though, because that was at noon, and now it's after three o'clock. And, um, you missed a few buttons." I looked down with horror to see the bottom two buttons of my shirt hanging wide open. Chris smacked the rolled set of plans he was holding against a bookcase and took off down the hall.

"Oh God, Chris. No! It's not like that!" I said, buttoning up. "He's just a friend who's having some problems with his wife. He's confused, but he's going back home!"

"So he's already on a plane, is that what you're telling me?"

asked Chris.

"Well, not exactly. Come here." I pulled him aside into an empty conference room. "But he'll be gone *soon*, and in the meantime he's getting his own room."

"His own room!" said Chris. "Well that makes me feel so much better! Look, Tessa, if you were seeing somebody back home you should've just told me." He stormed out of the conference room and back to his office.

"Hey," I said, following him. "I don't know what you're so upset about, it's not like you and I are dating or anything! We just hung out a few times!" What the hell was I even talking about? Of course we did more than just hang out. But sometimes there's no shutting me up.

"You're right about that," said Chris. "We are definitely not dating."

I should have just left at that point, but like I said, sometimes I just don't know when to shut up.

"What were you dropping off for me anyway?" I asked.

Chris banged something into his keyboard, staring straight ahead and refusing to look at me. "You're kidding me right?" he asked.

I stood there stupidly in his doorway for a few seconds before I noticed the dozen yellow roses peeking out of his trash can. If I felt any worse than I did at that moment I probably would've just thrown myself out the window.

"Oh," I said. I looked over at Dan for help, but his back was to me and he was pretending not to have heard anything. I went back to my office and shut the door.

Chris was right, after all. I was kidding him, I was kidding Nick, and I was kidding myself. I was trying to have everything, when in reality I didn't know what the hell I wanted. I felt sick as all my thoughts of staying in Vegas started to go up in smoke - and even sicker at the thought of returning to Massachusetts as nothing but a home-wrecking, loser, secretary.

20

"I can't believe you dragged me here."

I shook my head as we passed under a poster for Thunder From Down Under - the resident male strip show at The Excalibur hotel. Twelve chiseled, long-haired, somewhat orange-skinned men, standing in a row wearing nothing but black boy-shorts that looked like the bottom half of my Victoria's Secret pajamas.

Kendra whistled. "Hey, what better way to get your mind off your man troubles than with a bunch of hot naked men?" "They don't actually get naked, do they?" I asked in horror. I wasn't exactly sure what Kendra was into, but I certainly did not need to see *that* stuff flopping around.

"No, no," said Kendra, a tad disappointed. "Not naked. But it's totally hands-on." She winked at me and handed our tickets to the doorman.

"Oh dear lord."

I cringed as the host led us to our front row seats - this was a lot to stomach on a Tuesday night. I don't know what it is about hulking, gyrating, beefcakes that tends to turn me off, but I do know that I'm in the minority. While we waited for the show to begin, a documentary played showing what the dancers do in their free time on the ranch. You know, the ranch that they all live on together half naked. The men were riding horses shirtless. Some were riding pantless.

The woman seated next to me just about lost her mind when two of the men started rinsing off a horse. I sunk down a little further in my seat and prayed that she didn't try to talk to me. I mean, this was just her reaction to a *movie*. What the hell would her reaction be when the real live men came out? I did not have to wait long to find out. Before I knew it, Kendra was screaming along with the rest of the lunatics, and a man in a blue spandex thong came crawling on all fours down our table.

"Hey!" I yelled, as he knocked over my nine dollar beer with his knees. I looked across the table at Kendra, but her and all the other horn-dog women were too busy grabbing at the guy's body to even notice how he had just massacred our drinks. When he reached the end of the table he stood up, grabbed another woman's beer, and poured it down his chest, signaling the beginning of a thrust-off with the stripper at the next table.

I tolerated another four atrocious dance numbers before sneaking out to use the ladies room. *Maybe there's something wrong with me,* I thought as I sat on the toilet, folding and re-folding a square of toilet paper. *How come everybody else loves this shit?* All those oiled-up, sweaty, men did for me was make my chest tighten as I thought about Chris. Not because they reminded me of him in any shape or form, God no. Those guys could toss Chris around like a bale of hay. No, it was just the opposite. All the screaming and thrusting made me long for a cozy night of Monopoly. *Screw it.*

I pulled out my phone and dialed Chris's number, though I had no idea what I would say to him if he answered. Maybe I would just beg him to come rescue me again. But, not surprisingly, it rang four times and went to voicemail. I fought the impulse to dial him again, and headed sadly back into the theater where *It's Raining Men* was practically blowing the doors off.

"I got you something!" screamed Kendra, as I slid into my seat. She pointed to the deathly black Jaeger shot waiting for me on the table.

"Nobody kicked it over yet?" I shouted back.

"What?"

"Nothing."

"Whoooo!" she screamed, holding her own shot high into the air as one of the dancers back-flipped off the stage. "It's raining men!"

Hallelujah. I rolled my eyes and downed my shot.

***

I was holed up in my studio at Mocha Fresco on Friday afternoon, surrounded by warm sunshine streaming through the skylights and the smell of coffee. Kendra could not have picked a better week for my studio time to begin because in the current state of my life, I was enjoying having some quiet time to myself. Chris still hadn't spoken to me all week, even going so far as to enlist Roberta as his assistant. I wanted to laugh whenever I saw her in his doorway asking a million stupid questions, but then I remembered why she was there and there was really nothing funny about it.

I couldn't blame him for being angry with me. Every time I tried to tell Nick to go back home, I felt guilty as hell. I mean, he had left his wife after some stupid text messages that *I* started, and now I was going to tell him it was all a mistake? Then there was another part of me - a small, sick, twisted, part of me, that believed if I sent Nick away, I might be left with nobody.

Nobody.

And so I sat, thoughtfully cutting, and gluing, and analyzing my sad state of affairs. Honestly, I haven't even seen all that much of Nick over the past week. Tuesday night I went to the strip show and told him I had to work late. I snuck into my room smelling like a bottle of men's cologne from the 1990's and went straight to sleep. Wednesday night Kendra and I took him out to dinner and to see the pirate show at Treasure Island (where I totally by accident may have made out with him for like five seconds). And Thursday night he said that he "had plans." I know that one of those "plans" involved going to The Jiggly Kitty because I found a receipt for it in his hotel room.

But I decided not to ask questions. Who was I to say anything? Unlike Thunder from Down Under, the girls at The Jiggly Kitty at least stay up on stage and out of reach. I was dying, however, to ask him what he needed a receipt for - was he planning to get reimbursed? Oh the look on Margaret Sherman's face.

I washed the glue off my hands and walked out into the

coffee shop for a latte. I stopped short when I saw Nick already seated at the bar and talking with Holly. She giggled and leaned in toward him, tucking a piece of hot pink hair behind her ear. She was flirting of course, who could blame her? That part didn't bother me. That was nothing. But then, she pretended to drop his change onto the counter, and he playfully reached out and grabbed her by the wrist. She clenched the coins in her hand and he wrestled them out of her grip, both of them laughing hysterically. Now that, that was something.

"Small latte, please," I interrupted, sliding into the seat next to Nick.

"Let me know if I can get you anything else." Holly gave him a wink before she headed off to make my drink. I rolled my eyes.

"I didn't know you were coming here," I said. "What have you been up to today?"

Nick swiveled around on his bar stool to face me and leaned back, stretching. His shirt rose up a little revealing a tanned stomach from a week of lounging by the hotel pool. "Not much," he said. "Went to check out the view from the Stratosphere. Had lunch."

"By yourself?"

He looked at his watch. "I met some people."

"People?"

"Girls."

"You met some girls?"

"Four girls, on a bachelorette party. They were cool."

I took my coffee from Holly and motioned for him to follow me back to the studio. "You went to lunch with four girls?"

"Lunch and some sightseeing. No big deal."

"No big deal," I repeated. "Nick, what the hell are you doing?"

"What do you mean?" he asked, hopping up on the corner of my work table.

"I mean, you came to Las Vegas to see *me,* did you not? And now, I've barely seen you all week because you're out picking up girls."

"No, you haven't seen me all week because you've been avoiding me for some reason," said Nick. He inched his way down the table and put his hand on my waist. I wriggled free.

"I haven't been avoiding you," I lied. "You're just confusing me. You're married, you like me, you want to date other girls and go to strip clubs. What is your deal?"

He looked me in the eyes and put his hand on the back of my head. "My deal, Tessa, is that I'm in love with you. I know you have feelings for me too, you said so in those texts."

All the years, all the hints, and the only reason he had any clue about my feelings is because of a few drunken text messages. I felt sick.

"I have some feelings, Nick," I said. "Right now I feel that you need to get out of here." I ducked out from underneath his hand and walked over to the door. "Please just go, I can't deal."

"You're kicking me out again? This is what I get for telling you that I love you?"

"You don't love me."

"Then why would I have come to Las Vegas?"

"Because you're fighting with your wife and thought it would be fun to fool around with your old friend. Trust me, Nick, if you loved me, you would have figured it out a long time ago. Realizing it five minutes after I asked you what you were wearing is not love. And, by the way, it was my boss who sent you that one. Plus, if you loved me you wouldn't be out there flirting with Holly, and you certainly wouldn't be gallivanting around with four girls you just met."

"Whoa, whoa! Easy now," said Nick. "None of that is true."

"Oh, so you're saying that you do all those things to girls that you're in love with?" I rinsed a few paintbrushes out in the sink with more vigor than was necessary. "Real nice. I can't believe I was ever jealous of Megan."

"I knew you were jealous of Megan! You told me that if *you* were my wife you'd never let me leave the - "

"Oh God, Nick, please just stop!" I dropped the brushes into the sink and turned around to face him. "I know what I wrote. But can you honestly tell me that before any of those texts and emails happened, that you had ever given me a second thought...that way?"

We stood looking at each other in silence for what seemed like forever. I could tell that he wanted to say something, but that he also didn't want to lie to me.

"Well?"

"I should go," he said.

And without another word, he ducked his head and disappeared out the door. I wondered if Holly would follow him out to his car to make sure that he was okay. I didn't even care - she could have him. They could all have him. He looked different as I watched him leave - no longer the image of perfection that I had built him up to be in my mind.

He looked, to be honest, like any other guy.

21

"Look what the cat dragged in." I nudged Kendra with my elbow. We were leaning up against the bar at Pure inside Caesar's Palace, angry at the world, and downing Red Bull and vodkas at what some might call an alarming rate.

"Oh shit," she said.

We watched in horror as Rob Dorfman pushed his way through the crowd, followed by a man with sunken cheeks and a crew cut who I did not recognize. They seemed to be headed right for us. I glanced around for a pole or a really tall guy to hide behind, but there was nothing. And there was no time.

"Who's that other guy?" I asked, trying to avoid looking in their direction.

"Uh, only the biggest f - "

"Hey you!" I interrupted as Rob suddenly appeared right in front of us. Please understand that that is not the normal greeting I use for Rob when he comes into the office. But my vodka and I decided at the last minute that outside the office,

Rob is just another human being. And there is no reason that I should be afraid of another human being.

"Whatcha doing here?" I asked.

Both of them looked from me to Kendra, and then their eyes lowered about six inches. I rolled my eyes. Kendra had on one of her racier tops, not to mention the short shorts and silver stilettos. When we left her house that evening I told her that she may as well have worn a pair of nylon basketball shorts since nobody's eyes were going to make it past her chest. Point proven. I actually have a theory about Kendra's choice of clothing and her encounters with her husband, Todd. It seems that the worse the encounter, the less clothing she wears out to the bars. It's a pretty perfect correlation.

Today, for example, Todd stopped by the house to borrow the luggage that he and Kendra had received as a wedding present, so that he could take Carlotta to Hawaii. Hawaii is also the place where Kendra and Todd happen to have honeymooned. Eight hours later, there were her boobs, on full display. The correlation never failed.

"Um," said Rob. I have never before heard the man hesitate. "Uh." He finally pried his eyes off of Kendra and looked at me. I was slightly offended that his eyes remained firmly on my face. "This is Jasper, Jasper Quick, from the Riverlin Zoning Commission. We're just having a little boys night out."

"Nice to meet you," I said. Jasper shook my hand while keeping one eye on Kendra.

Jasper Quick! The pervert Chris and Dan had told me about. Why the heck was he having a "boys night out" with Rob? There was at least a twenty year age difference between the two of them. Rob was a jerk, but I was pretty sure he had jerky friends his own age that he could be hanging out with on a Saturday night.

"Cool," I said. "You boys certainly do need to let loose once in a while."

I mentally told myself to stop referring to them as "boys." For some reason, it made me feel like taking a shower. But I needed to say *something* since Kendra still hadn't spoken a word to either of them. She just stood there awkwardly sucking down her Red Bull. I don't know what I expected her to say anyway, I mean here was a man who had told her countless times that she was an incompetent idiot, and now he was invading her personal life. Never mind that Jasper referred to her as "sweet cheeks" whenever she appeared before the Commission.

I followed Jasper's gaze as it moved from Kendra to a bachelorette party that had just entered the bar. Before I even knew what was happening, he had ditched us and resurfaced in the center of their group. The girls were unfortunately too drunk to scatter. I stood there watching him in disgust until Rob bumped into my elbow as he sidled in closer to us. His yellow button up shirt and sweater vest were a stark contrast with the trendy atmosphere inside the club.

"I didn't realize that loafers were part of the dress code," I said.

"What?"

"I said I didn't realize that Stouffers made pie a la mode!"

"Yeah, whatever," said Rob. He took a swig of beer and turned his back to me.

Jasper was now posing for pictures with who I assumed to be the bachelorette. He sort of reminded me of Tooth Model. The world might implode on itself if those two ever bumped into each other - at least I hoped it would, for its own sake.

"Look at the old pervert!" Kendra suddenly broke her silence by shouting directly into Rob's face. "I hope those girls enjoy getting ROOFIED!"

I grabbed her by the arm as she lost her balance and nearly fell into Rob, shooting her my best "shut up you idiot we're in front of a client" look, but it went right over her head. I shouldn't have been so concerned because when I stole a glance at Rob he seemed to be enjoying himself immensely. He slid an arm around Kendra's waist, a goofy smile on his face.

"You don't like Jasper very much, do you?" He was almost eye level with her chest.

"That man," she said, pointing a finger into Rob's face, "has no respect for women. *None*! And -" She paused to throw back a shot that she grabbed from a passing waitress. "At one of our hearings he said we'd get his vote only if *I* was going to be working at The Jiggly Kitty. *Me*! A stripper! Canyoubelieveit?" Her last four words ran together in one drunken slur.

"I hope you don't think those terrible things about me too," said Rob putting his arm around Kendra's shoulders and speaking in a baby voice that made me want to grind my heel into his stupid loafers.

"Of course not!" Kendra put her arm around Rob's waist. "You see, *you*, are a gentleman, and you only do the things you do because you need to get by in this ridiculous business." Her finger was pointing all around again. "Sometimes you have to be mean in order to get what you want. That's what *I've* learned. Right Tessa?"

Rob - a gentleman? I gave a half-hearted shrug, unsure of where she was going with this rant, and not ready to applaud Rob for treating us like dirt.

"All I'm saying," she continued, "is that Todd wanted Carlotta, so what did he do? He dumped me. *Totally* mean. But it got him what he wanted. So good for him. Good for *fucking* him!"

Rob nodded along in agreement, looking seriously into her eyes. For some reason him looking into her eyes made me feel sicker than when he stared at her chest.

"I'm glad that we have an understanding," he said. "Because I was hoping you ladies might be willing to do me a small favor."

"What's that?" I asked.

"Well, Jasper took some of his own personal time to come out with me tonight, and we were fortunate enough to have run into you two single ladies. I was hoping maybe you could help me show him a good time."

"A good time?" I asked.

"Yes, you know - dance with a him a little bit, make him feel special."

"Um, he seems to be having a pretty good time on his own," I said.

A woman in stonewashed jeans and a jet black perm, who had materialized out of the 1990's, was grinding her backside into Jasper's front side while running her hands down his face. Kendra and I crinkled our noses in unison.

"True," said Rob, "but unfortunately that lady's name doesn't appear on my zoning application." He took a long slimy sip from his beer.

"Neither does mine," I said.

"That is also true," said Rob.

"Actually, you two," interrupted Kendra, sounding as if she had just solved the mystery of the universe, "*my* name is on that application. Kendra Stoltz, Professional Engineer! *P.E.* You know what P.E. really stands for? Pretty Fucking Entertaining! Yeah, I'll do it. If that bastard thinks I'm a stripper, well then I wouldn't want to disappoint him!"

"Ken, please," I said. "How is *that* going to punish him?"

Kendra ignored me and started readjusting her boobs.

"That's right," said Rob, "show him how much fun you are. Make him fall in love with you. Then once he approves our application you can break his heart by never speaking to him again. I get what I want, you get what you want, everybody wins!"

"That's the stupidest thing I ever heard!" I shouted. "Don't listen to him!"

"No! This is *my* company and I need to do what's best for it," said Kendra. "This is what my parents wanted me to do with my life isn't it? Daddy would be *so* proud. Thank goodness I'm not out there painting pictures because *that* would be disgraceful!"

Before either of us could say another word Kendra was out

on the dance floor fighting the 90's time warp lady for Jasper's attention and whispering God knows what into his ear. I couldn't take the sight of it. I may be indecisive and somewhat of a pushover, but I will never be a sell-out. Especially not for Rob Dorfman and this shitty company. I stood there shaking my head and fuming while Rob stared at me.

"What?" I finally asked.

"Care to keep a client happy?" he asked, motioning for me to join him and his vibrant sweater vest on the dance floor. Every muscle in my face tightened as I informed him, through clenched teeth, that I had irrevocably converted to lesbianism.

***

I stormed out of Caesar's Palace leaving Kendra, Jasper, and Rob to have a three-way for all I cared. Rob was a despicable little worm, so no big surprises there. But for Kendra to actually go along with his sick ideas? I felt bad for leaving her in there, but if that's what she wanted I couldn't exactly drag her out against her will.

I stood there rather drunk on the sidewalk, watching two cross-dressers get out of a taxi. They shouted at the driver in Spanish, one of them tossing a mane of long black hair over his shoulder and flinging a bunch of bills through the passenger side window. The driver peeled off, just missing a group of girls who had spilled out of the hotel and into the road. Never a dull moment in this place.

I flipped open my phone and stared at the screen, unsure of what to do with it. This was the second time that Kendra had ditched me to hook up with a guy, but at least the first time had led to my getting together with Chris. This time I had nothing. Just a headache and some early signs of depression. I missed Chris. I wanted to go to the arcade again - I wanted to go on a second date with him for Christ's sake. But I could have none of those things until Nick was out of my life. I scrolled through my list of Contacts until I came to Trask.

I called Nick and asked him to meet me at Sweet Dreams, a little dessert and coffee shop a few doors down The Strip. There we could sit down in a quiet, *public*, place, with no alcohol, and no beds, and we could end this shit once and for all.

After about twenty minutes a taxi pulled up and deposited a tanned and refreshed looking Nick Trask onto the sidewalk. His little vacation that was ruining my life was certainly doing wonders for his appearance. *It doesn't matter what he looks like!* I scolded myself. *He lied to you, remember?* I had three Red Bull and vodka's pumping through my veins and my determination was at an all time high. If I couldn't put my foot down and send him home tonight, then it was probably never going to happen.

"You look nice," said Nick, as we followed the hostess to a table in the back of the dimly lit restaurant.

"Thanks." I was suddenly very aware that I was wearing a tube top and that my arms were covered in glitter. Not exactly restaurant attire. I tried to casually brush some off with my hands as we ordered two slices of chocolate cheesecake. I wasn't so sure how well Red Bull and vodka would mix with chocolate cheesecake, but puking in front of Nick might lessen his desire for me, so I went ahead with the order.

"Do you remember the time," I asked, when the waitress had left us, "that our office took that field trip to The Jiggly Kitty after it opened in Leominster? It was like two o'clock in the afternoon."

"And Donna Spang's husband was in there," said Nick laughing.

"Getting a lap dance," I added. "How's she doing anyway? Still about three seconds away from destroying the universe?"

"She's pretty busy, actually. I think Tom's running her into the ground."

"That's too bad," I said. "Guess her twelve year streak of doing nothing and getting paid for it is coming to an end."

"She had a good run," said Nick. "So, uh, besides Donna Spang, what did you want to talk about? You look like you were in the middle of a fun night." He gestured to my arm glitter.

Okay, Tessa. It's go time. I took a deep breath and looked Nick seriously in the face.

"You're right," I said. "I didn't ask you here to talk about old times. I have something important that I need to tell you."

But Nick didn't seem to hear me as he had already been distracted by a man seated at the table to our left making a lot of strange sounds with his throat.

"Sir, are you okay?" asked Nick.

"Well," said the man, "in all honesty I'm just having a bit of trouble belching."

Oh dear lord. I buried my face in my hands.

"Really?" asked Nick, intrigued. That is the type of thing that intrigues him.

"Waitress!" said the man. "Do you think I could get a

pickle over here? I think if I had a pickle it would help me to belch."

"Nick," I said. "Are you listening to me?"

"We don't serve pickles here, sir," said the waitress. "This is a dessert shop."

"Nick," I said again, kicking him under the table. "I don't think this guy needs our help. I have something important to tell you."

Nick looked at me for a few seconds and then turned back to the pickle guy. "What is it about a pickle that you think would help?"

Burping pickle guy did not respond right away because he was pounding himself on the chest. "I just have a feeling, you know? Sometimes you just have to go with your instincts." Burping pickle guy had a point.

"Nick," I said for the third time. "He does have a point. Sometimes you need to go with your instincts, and my instincts are telling me that -" Just as I was about to finally speak my mind, Nick's phone began to ring and he looked down at the caller ID.

"Shit," he mumbled and looked guiltily up at me. "It's Megan." He stuck the phone back into his pocket. "What were you saying?"

"I was *saying* that sometimes something that you think is what you wanted, turns out to -" This time I was interrupted by his phone beeping a text message alert. He looked at it and swore again, this time louder.

"Uh, Tess," he said, looking nervously all over the restaurant, "that was Megan again. She's, uh, she's *here*."

22

"She's *here?*" I shouted. Burping pickle guy turned to look at me. "Here *where?*"

"Here, Las Vegas. At the airport. Well, maybe at the airport, I don't really know."

"Well what did her message say?"

"Um, it said *'found u you son of a bitch. See u in ten.*"

"Oh dear lord. See you in ten? Ten minutes? How did she find your hotel?"

"She's very good with the Internet," said Nick.

"Alright, it's okay," I said, trying not to panic. "You just need to get back to the hotel to meet her, and I'll just go stay far away at Kendra's house." I started gathering up my purse and getting money out to pay the bill.

"The thing is, Tess, I think she may be coming *here* here. To this restaurant."

I stopped counting out the tip and glared at him. "And

how on Earth would she know that you're *here*?"

"Because I kind of told the front desk clerk," he said.

"The front desk clerk? The one with the boob job?"

"Are there other front desk clerks?" he asked. "I never noticed. She asked me where I would be later tonight."

"So let me get this straight, you were flirting with the front desk clerk before you came here to cheat on your wife with the girl you claim to be in love with? Christ, Nick, what the hell is wrong with you?"

Before he had a chance to explain to me what the hell was wrong with him, two things happened. First, burping pickle guy let out the loudest belch I've heard in years, and second, the door to Sweet Dreams flew open to reveal Megan Trask, fresh off of her cross-country flight. A flash of lightning and an axe in her hand would have completed the scene, but she had apparently brought nothing, not even a carry-on bag. This was a woman on a mission. My life flashed before my eyes as she came charging through the restaurant to our table.

"There you are you lying sack of crap!" she shouted. "Did you think I was going to just let my husband disappear for a week, no questions asked, and then wheel out the fucking welcome wagon when you finally decided to come home?"

"Megan, baby - " interrupted Nick.

"Don't you dare 'baby' me! I always knew something was going on with you two, I knew it! All those times you told me you were just friends, and that you thought Tessa was ugly, I never really bought it!"

Nick told his wife that he thought I was ugly? *Hey!*

"It's true, Meg! She's not even close to my type - "

"Save it!" shouted Megan. "You're going back to the hotel, and you're packing up your shit, and then you're coming home with me. We'll get a God damned divorce if that's what you want, but you're sure as hell not staying out here."

I shrunk down a few inches in my seat out of sheer terror as I knew she would be unleashing the wrath on me at any moment.

"Megan, baby," said Nick, standing up and putting his hand on Megan's shoulder, "just listen to me, please! There's nothing going on between Tessa and I. I just needed to talk with her about some things! About *us*."

"Ever hear of a phone?" asked Megan. She turned and looked around at the dimly lit restaurant, motioning to the candles on the tables. "This is where you go to talk? And at, what the hell time is it, one o'clock in the morning? Do you think I'm stupid?"

"Tessa asked me to meet her here!" said Nick. "She thinks that she's in love with me! I only showed up to try and let her down easy. I was just about to tell her that I needed to go home to you and that she needs to move on with her life, isn't that right, Tessa?"

I couldn't believe my ears. The bastard was throwing me under the bus! Did he honestly think I would cover for him like that?

"No, *Nick*," I sad, really emphasizing his name. "That's not right. Why would you do this to me?" I stood up and turned to Megan. "Megan, listen to me. I have a boyfriend. Well, I almost had a boyfriend, until Nick showed up and ruined everything."

"Hey!" said Nick.

"Shut up," said Megan and I in unison.

I turned to Nick and looked him dead in the eyes.

"I was in love with you for years, Nick, *years.* Not a couple of weeks, not since I sent those texts and emails, but *years.* Did you know that?" He shook his head and I turned to Megan who gave me a look that will probably follow me to my grave. "This started way before he ever met you," I assured her. I turned back to Nick with shaking hands.

"Knowing that I would see you, that was the only thing that got me into work every morning. Even when you went through that phase of only dating girls from the modeling agency, I sat and I listened to you talk about your dates, and I let you complain to me when they didn't work out. Do you know why I did that? Because it didn't matter to me what you were saying, all that mattered was that you were talking to *me.* I got to hear your voice and your jokes and at least for that moment, sitting in the middle of our stupid office, I was the girl in your life."

"Tessa, I'm -" interrupted Nick.

"No, let me finish," I said. "I know that sounds kind of creepy and stalker-ish, but I'm sorry. That's just the way it was. All those times that I comforted you while you dated idiot after idiot, and I kept telling you that the right girl was out there. I told you that when you least expected it she would show up. But you never once considered that girl might be me." I looked down at my cheesecake, and then at Megan, whose face had softened slightly. "And then one day he came back from a cruise, and he was married to you. All my hope was gone. I had to accept the fact that I was destined to be nothing but Nick's friend for the rest of my life, and it was devastating. I hated you, Megan, for no good reason. I took all my anger at Nick and I placed it squarely on you, just like every other bitter, jealous, woman does, and I'm so sorry about that. I want to be better than that."

Tears formed in my eyes, but I kept on talking. "At the time I would have given anything for your marriage to end and for me to get that glimmer of hope back. That hope that someday Nick would come to his senses and we would end up together."

"Tess, I didn't -" interrupted Nick again.

"I'm not *done*," I said. "And then I came out here, and I met this really great guy who I never told you about. I should have, because he's everything you never could be, and by not telling you about him I may have royally messed it all up."

"Then why would you send me those texts?" asked Nick, finally getting a few words in. He spoke almost in a whisper, as if he didn't want Megan to hear.

"Because when you told me that you and Megan were having problems, a little piece of that old stalker was still hanging on. I just couldn't let her go." I shrugged. "It's like when you're ten years old and your parents finally buy you that toy you wanted when you were eight - you know, you play with it for a while, but then you realize that it's not what you really want anymore."

The entire restaurant, including wait staff, seemed to hold their breath as I finished my speech.

"I'm not in love with your husband anymore," I said to Megan. The words sounded so liberating to my own ears, I wanted to shout them to the entire city. "It was just kind of nice that finally, after all these years, Nick thought that he was in love with *me.*" I gave Nick a weak smile and shrugged. Then I sat back down. "That's all."

Burping pickle guy, along with everybody else who had been listening intently, let out a collective murmur of agreement, and then, just like in a movie, slowly began to clap.

The sound of applause seemed to bring Megan out of the daze from which she had been listening to me, wide eyed and unblinking. She jerked her head up and down in what I hoped was a sign of forgiveness, or at least a sign that she wasn't going to rip my heart out of my throat.

"This is unreal," she murmured under her breath. She looked up at her husband, and, having the final word in the matter, told him that it was time to go.

I half expected her to drag Nick out by his earlobe, but he willingly trailed after her, hands jammed into his pockets. Before they exited the restaurant he turned and mouthed something to me. Maybe it was "sorry," or "help me," but in the dim light I couldn't be sure.

People were still clapping, whistling even, as if I has just put on the performance of a lifetime. I knew somewhere inside me was relief and pride at what I had just done, but at the moment neither of those things were able to break through the utterly depressing thought of being left alone at the table with two plates of half eaten cheesecake and cold coffee.

Burping pickle guy muttered something to me about "what happens in Vegas stays in Vegas," and I told him that if he didn't want a certain part of his anatomy to remain in Vegas he would mind his own business. I gathered up my stuff as quickly as I could, nodded appreciation to my fans, and headed out to the street to look for a taxi. I saw Nick and Megan standing at the curb to the right, so I headed left as fast as my legs would take me.

***

Kendra's house was dark when the taxi dropped me off. I pulled the spare key out from under a potted palm on the back porch and let myself in, making sure to turn off the security system. The last thing I needed was to make another scene tonight. The guest bedroom was on the first floor and I stumbled into it, not bothering to turn on the lights. Clothes and all I fell into bed and pulled the covers up over my head. I took my cell phone out of my pocket, the numbers glowing green under the covers.

"Hello?"

"Hey, Kara," I said. "I think he's on his way."

***

Someone was crawling into bed with me.

"Mmmmmmpphh," they mumbled into the pillow.

"Kendra? Is that you?" I whispered. I couldn't get my eyes to focus in the dark. I hoped to hell it was her, otherwise I was in trouble.

"Mmmmmhmmmmmph," they said.

"How did you know I was in here? What time is it?" I sat up on my elbow. At least the mumbling seemed to be female.

"You dropped your purse in the hall. It's like six a.m. I

think I'm gonna be sick."

"Um, okay, can you give me a little warning first?"

"Mmmmmmph."

I laid back down and stared into the darkness. The curtains in the guest room were so thick that an atomic bomb could go off in the backyard and you wouldn't see a thing. A vampire could watch The Price is Right at eleven o'clock in the morning in this room and be totally fine. *Six a.m.* The night before started to slowly come back to me. I had left Kendra with Rob and Jasper and proceeded to either ruin or fix Nick's marriage, I wasn't quite sure. Now it was six a.m. and Kendra was just getting home. *Oh no*! I sat back up and shook her.

"Ken! Wake up!" I said. "Please tell me you didn't just now get back from showing Jasper a good time?"

"I said I felt sick, didn't I?" she mumbled.

"Oh God. That's so gross."

"At least we'll be getting our zoning approved."

"You realize he's only one of seven Board members don't you? He still has to convince the other six. Or did you sleep with all of them?" I asked.

"I'm such a slut."

"No, you're not. You were drunk. I never should have left you there." Another repulsive thought entered my mind. I was almost afraid to ask, and maybe if there was some light in the room so I could see her face, I wouldn't have. "You didn't do anything with Rob did you?" I scrunched my face up in the dark, expecting the worst.

"Ugh, no way. Once the little pervert saw that I was all

over Jasper he crawled back into whatever hole he comes out of in the morning and I never saw him again."

"Good," I said. "Because if you sleep with Rob Dorfman it's kind of the law that I have to murder you. Sleeping with Jasper just earns you a mild beating." I punched her under the covers.

"Please just murder me anyway. This is bad Tess, this is *really* bad. I think I might have a serious problem."

"So sleeping with Jasper was rock bottom for you?" I asked.

"Sleeping with Jasper would be rock bottom for a prostitute," said Kendra.

"What about sleeping with Rob?"

"That would be rock bottom for the pink algae that grows out of your shower head."

"You have pink algae growing out of your shower head? I thought someone with your money would have a maid."

Kendra ignored me. "God I need a shower. Jasper fucking Quick! How thick were my beer goggles?"

"You had a pretty good set going," I said. "So, uh, did he live up to his name?"

"I couldn't even tell you, honestly. And don't try to make me remember, I'd rather not."

"If you think about it he's really not that much worse than Phil Baxter, and you find Phil Baxter sexy. You told me so."

"Do *not* put him in the same category as Phil. You know how I feel about him." The sheets rustled as she rolled over onto her back, or maybe her stomach. I still couldn't see in the dark.

"I'm just teasing," I said. "But seriously, you agree with me now that we need to cool it with the drinking?"

"I...am...never...drinking...again," said Kendra.

"Give me your hand." I waved mine around in the dark. I found it and she limply shook with me on the deal. "Tomorrow morning, which I guess is right now, we're going to start over as respectable people. We'll give your house a good cleaning, starting with those shower heads, and then we'll go to the spa and get one of those cleansing treatments, you know, like Tom Cruise gets."

"What the heck are you talking about?" Kendra mumbled into her pillow.

I ignored her. I knew exactly what I was talking about. A fresh start. No more hangovers, no more pining away for Nick Trask. And at the center of my fresh start was Chris - hopefully still waiting for me to make up my mind. Megan, the woman I had wasted so much energy on hating, had done me a huge favor by showing up and taking Nick away. What doesn't kill us makes us stronger, they say. And Megan, to my surprise, hadn't killed me.

23

He's not coming.

I glanced down at my watch and checked my cell phone for the billionth time. Sunday was a busy day at the bumper boats and with every passing minute I prayed that nobody else would sit down on our bench. That was *his* spot and it needed to be empty when he showed up. He was now ten minutes late and hadn't even replied to my text message asking him to meet me here, so I was starting to get nervous.

Five more minutes passed. Since the time we had last shared this bench somebody had broken one of the legs so that it wobbled dangerously under my weight, but I didn't care. Until somebody pried it out of the cement and threw it into the bumper boats I was not going to budge, and even then Chris might find me smiling and waving as I slowly sank to the bottom of the pool. That is if he showed up at all. Which he would. He just had to.

It was 11:30 a.m. when I finally crawled out of bed that morning, Kendra's guest room still a pit of darkness. Kendra was still asleep, snoring lightly, and I tip-toed out of the room allowing her a few more minutes of peace before awakening to a lifetime of the fact that she had slept with Jasper Quick. My big plans of cleaning and spa treatments were scrapped when I realized how late it was. As soon as I had showered I sent Chris a text. *Bumper boats in twenty? Please?* I didn't wait for a reply, I just got into my car and headed over on faith. As I drove I thought about the short list of guys I had found myself in love with over the years.

I dated my first love, Sam, for three years in high school, fooling around in the art room after school behind leftover props from Jesus Christ Superstar. We thought we would be together forever. Being fifteen years old we were *grown-ups* for God's sake, how could anything ever change between us? We even went off to the same college, but it wasn't long before Sam turned into a beer guzzling frat boy who actually allowed other men to spank him on the ass with a paddle, and refused to tell me any details of his initiation.

I watched in horror as the Sam I loved and had planned my entire future with turned into somebody I would not even choose to be friends with. His room in the frat house was despicable and I refused to sleep over, which may have been the reason he found several other girls who *were* willing to sleep over. But it was okay, because giving up your independence to become a mindless lemming was unacceptable to me.

I soon discovered that college was a big place full of new guys and new art rooms to fool around in. Dorm rooms too. We broke up two months into our second semester, and so followed a parade of mostly unremarkable boyfriends and the occasional walk of shame. Eventually I was spat out into the real world, still alone, and three years shy of meeting the second love of my life, Nick Trask. I do not need to tell you how that one turned out.

The third try would be a charm, I just knew it. The only catch was that Chris needed to show up. I was about thirty seconds away from drowning my sorrows in a bag of cotton candy, when my end of the bench rose up like a see-saw as somebody much heavier sat down next to me.

"You come here often?" asked Chris.

Just the sound of his voice began to magically dissolve the weight that had been parked on my chest for the past week.

"I do, actually," I said. "This lame guy I know thinks it's cool to bring girls here."

"You want to hear lame? I used to come here with a girl who makes stick figures out of paperclips."

"Sounds like genius to me."

A refreshing mist from the bumper boats blew over us, reminding me that I had been waiting in the sun for nearly half an hour in what felt like 150 degree temperatures. My arms were already quite red. I stole a sidelong glance at Chris, but he was staring straight ahead.

"So, um, that guy Nick, he's gone now," I said, determined not to waste another minute. "I, um, I made it quite clear to him that I met somebody else. Plus his wife flew in last night to get him. It was kind of a big scene."

"Yeah?" Chris looked over at me for the first time in a week.

"Yeah. It was pretty humiliating, actually. But I deserved it. I even deserved the week of silent treatment that you've been giving me. I mean, I had a crush on Nick for years, and you can't be mad at me for that because I didn't even know you then. But when he showed up here I should have sent him home. I should have told him about us right away, but I didn't. I'm so sorry, Chris. I was a stupid, idiot, moron."

"Nah," said Chris, leaning forward to rest his elbows on his knees. "I overreacted. Like you said, we weren't even officially dating and I got all psycho possessive over you." He tilted his head and looked at me sideways. "We've barely even known each other a month, do you realize that?"

"Of course," I said, starting to worry about what he was getting at. "It's only been a month, so if you don't want to - "

"It's only been a month," he cut in, "and I already can't stand the thought of not being with you."

I felt my cheeks get warm without any help from the sun, and then even warmer as Chris leaned in to kiss me.

"Nothing happened between Nick and I, just so you know," I said quietly.

Chris ran his hand through his hair and looked at my sheepishly. "So, stopping off at the Bunny Ranch on my way here was a bad idea?"

"Yes!" I playfully jabbed him in the stomach. "Even though I probably would have deserved it! Oh Chris, I can't believe I almost messed all of this up. I've never met anybody before who was so much -" I struggled to find the words. "Well, who was so much like *me.* You're *me* but you're a boy! How often does *that* happen?" I shook my head. "What an idiot I was. You should just fling me into the bumper boats."

"As much as I would love to watch you sail through the air," said Chris, "how about we just forget any of this ever happened?"

"Deal," I said. I sidled a bit closer to him on the bench and we sat in silence, thinking over what had been said, and soaking up each other's company which we had missed all week.

"So," said Chris, "want to ride the boats?"

"Ride them? You mean instead of just sitting here trash talking everybody?" I looked at him in mock horror, which wasn't one hundred percent mock. I wasn't exactly dressed for water sports with my brand new sneakers and thin white tank top.

"Sure, let's get nuts. Maybe we've been missing out on something great."

"But I'll get all wet!" I said.

"And the problem is?" He raised his eyebrows and gave me a devilish grin. "Come on."

I stepped over puddles as I followed him to the ticket counter, cringing at the thought of how wet and dirty they were about to become. But sneakers be damned, I would have followed him anywhere at that moment.

***

Over the next few weeks life took a turn for the better for all three of us. Chris and I were in that mushy romantic phase that some, myself included, might refer to as obnoxious. I had the luxury, however, of knowing that underneath all the mush lay plenty of substance, and that in due time substance would take over. There was no sense in rushing it.

Kendra held true to her word and laid off the alcohol and

the late nights, though my desire to spend time with Chris rather than packed into sweaty bars may have contributed to her success. Sometimes the three of us would go out to dinner or play miniature golf while Kendra eternally worried about being the third wheel. "If I ever become a pain in the ass, just tell me to get lost," she kept reminding Chris and I. We always reassured her that we would. But in private we agreed that she was still our boss, and telling our boss to get lost probably wasn't in our best interest. Still, we usually didn't mind the company.

I was also spending two nights a week in my studio at Mocha Fresco, and on a whim one afternoon took a rather tacky Las Vegas themed wall clock that I had made over to one of the local gift shops. I plunked it down on the counter.

"What's this?" the shop owner asked, as if he wasn't already surrounded by piles of tacky Las Vegas crap.

"It's a clock," I said. "I made it myself. I was wondering if you bought and sold stuff from, um, from local artists?"

The owner picked up my work and turned it around in his hands, inspecting it like an art critic, holding it up to the light and peering at it from all angles. While I waited for him to finish I looked over the racks of Bud Light t-shirts and rolled my eyes. I pulled a cat figurine, complete with fake fur and vacant marble eyes, off a shelf and held it up in front of him. "Did you inspect these the same way?"

He laughed. "You've got me there, but the thing is, those cats get pumped in from China and cost me less than two bucks." I flipped the cat over to read the price tag. $6.95.

"To be honest with you, sir, I haven't sold *anything* before." I put the cat back on the shelf and looked the owner square in the eye. "I will give you this thing for free if you want. All I ask is that you put it on a shelf with a price tag and let me know if anybody buys it. Please?"

"I'm sorry, miss, but I don't really sell this type of thing here. Why don't you go to the Bellagio? They sell art over there. Me? I sell -" he motioned to the cat figurines.

"I know," I said. "But look at it, the clock part came from Wal-Mart. I made the rest of it out of bottle caps and post cards. Do you really think this thing would sell at the Bellagio? Come on, it's tacky, but it's not bad. What have you got to lose?" I almost heard a little Rob Dorfman in my voice - Rob Dorfman the businessman, not Rob Dorfman the douchebag.

The owner shrugged and rolled his eyes. "Okay, fine. Ten dollars."

"You're going to pay me?"

"Of course I'm going to pay you. I give you ten, I sell it for twenty, everybody wins."

"You think somebody would pay twenty dollars for this?" I asked.

"I sure as hell wouldn't," he said. "But tourists buy some strange stuff. If this thing doesn't sell though, you and I never do business again."

"Thank you!" I said, grabbing his hand and pumping it up and down. "I would love the opportunity to possibly never do business with you again!"

I returned to the store two days later and walked up and down the aisles trying to find where he had displayed it, but I found nothing.

"Hey, little lady!" the owner called out to me from a back room. "I was hoping you'd come back."

"Where's my clock?" I asked, walking to the front counter, half expecting to see my creation poking out of the trash can.

"It sold."

"It sold?" I asked, disbelieving.

"Sure did," he said. "This guy thought it was great. 'Like nothing he'd ever seen before' were the words he used. Told me he's going to hang it up in his office. I really talked you up too, I told him that once you're dead that thing will be worth a *lot*."

"One can only hope!" I said.

Why had I never tried to sell anything before? Did it really just take a little bit of effort? All those things they tell you as a kid about "being anything that you want to be," it couldn't possibly be true could it? I mean, that would be cra -

"I don't think we've been properly introduced," said the owner, interrupting my thoughts. "My name's Leo."

"Tessa Golden," I said.

"So, Tessa Golden, you got any more of this crap?"

24

The second I got out to the street I called Chris to tell him the news. It had been exciting in itself when the store owner bought my lousy clock, but now a person who I did not know would have my work on display in their office. In the context of my life, this was a truly unbelievable turn of events, and all it had taken was a little bit of initiative. I bought myself a frozen margarita-by-the-yard to celebrate and stood watching the gondolas outside the Venetian. If I had a hat I would have tossed it in the air, Mary Tyler Moore style.

With this newfound optimism, I approached Kendra for the second time with the idea of starting our own art business together. But again she turned me down. She was in a fairly stable place in her life, quietly seeing Bryce Storm who, to all of our surprise, had called her for a second date a few weeks after their one night stand.

Things in the engineering world were running smoothly, and she had heard from Rob Dorfman that Jasper Quick was in the process of getting our zoning approved. She would still need years of therapy to recover from spending the night with him, but at least it was not for nothing. I was happy that she was happy, and I did not want to push her further. But the tiny bit of success I'd had at the gift shop left me with a nagging for more, and my days spent at the office filing and copying were becoming more and more unbearable.

I was also left with the nagging thought that it was already March, and I had only a few weeks left before Marisa was to return from maternity leave, and I was to return to Massachusetts. Chris and I discussed it on occasion, listing the pros and cons of a long distance relationship. There were certainly more cons than pros. If I was going to put in for a permanent transfer to the Vegas office, I would need to do it soon, and even then there was doubt as to whether they would have a position for me. If they didn't, and I still chose to stay, I would need to begin searching for another job. The thought of starting over as an administrative assistant at a new company and continuing the cycle I had fallen into nearly five years ago, made me nauseous.

"I can't do it, Chris, I can't," I said over a late Mexican dinner one evening. I stabbed at my enchiladas, watching the orange cheese squish out. "I don't want to move out here just to end up in another dead end job."

"So quit," he said. "Do something else."

"But that's all I know how to do! I could make like twenty bucks a week if I keep selling to the gift shop. I don't know about you, but I can't live off twenty bucks a week."

"I'm sure Rob could hook you up with a part-time job at The Jiggly Kitty."

"*That* joke never gets old." I rolled my eyes. "But hey, maybe that's what I'm meant to do. Dancing every night, probably on drugs, guys throwing money at me. It might not be so bad."

"And thanks to Flamhauser-Geist," said Chris, "traffic flow is phenomenal. You'll never have trouble parking."

"Exactly. Parking concerns have always held me back from a career in stripping." I squished more cheese out of my enchilada. All joking aside, the decision becoming clearer to me each day was that I should remain in Las Vegas. The only question was how I could make the most of this change that I'd been waiting for possibly my entire life.

We headed out to the street after dinner, stopping to watch the dancing waters at the Bellagio. I respectfully waited until the last strains of Viva Las Vegas played through the speakers, and the fountain went silent, before flipping open my vibrating phone. I had one new text message.

meet me at the kitty very important

It was from Kendra and that was all it said. Meet her at The Jiggly Kitty. Very important. I showed the message to Chris who rolled his eyes.

"What the heck do you think she's doing there?" I asked.

"It's probably her and Bryce's idea of an interesting date," said Chris. "You want to go?"

"Not particularly," I said. "But she said it's important. Let me text her back and see what she wants." We hung around on the sidewalk for ten more minutes waiting for a reply, but nothing ever came.

"It's on our way home," said Chris. "We can just stop in. I won't look, I promise."

As we walked to Chris's car in the Bellagio garage, I

thought over the reasons that Kendra could possibly want me to meet her at a seedy strip club.

"What if Tooth Model commandeered her phone and is waiting for me in the parking lot?" I asked.

"I'll take him down," said Chris. "I've been working out. Tearing up my pecs, wailing on my glutes." He stopped in his tracks and flexed his ass muscles in my direction, causing me to spit a mouthful of beer onto the trunk of his car. I was still laughing fifteen minutes later when we pulled into The Jiggly Kitty and had trouble finding a place to park.

"What happened to phenomenal traffic flow?" I asked, noticing that some cars had parked on the grass.

Chris gave me a rude gesture with his finger. "Dan designed this one."

"Nice," I said, "throw your friend under the bus. Oh hey look, there's Kendra's car. They usually take Bryce's Jag when they go out. Weird."

"What do you think we should take honey, the Beamer or the Jag?" Chris did a killer impression of Bryce as he squeezed into a space that was much too small for his SUV. "Well I did just take the Beamer to the bank this morning," he switched over to his Kendra voice as he straightened out the wheels. "Tough life."

I sucked in my stomach and squeezed out of the car, not telling Chris that I left a little bit of his paint job on the other driver's door. It was a beautiful evening and I kind of wished that Chris and I were headed somewhere romantic, and not into a strip joint where several pairs of bouncy breasts, none of them mine, were about to be plunged into his face.

It would have been a perfect evening to hang out on Kendra's patio by the pool with some drinks and some candles, maybe a little Bob Marley on the stereo. It was such a nice place to relax that I wouldn't even mind if Kendra and Bryce joined us. *Maybe I'll suggest it when we find them*, I thought, looking up at Chris's face and trying to judge whether or not he was looking forward to going inside this place. I know he promised not to look, but come on, men are men. I linked my arm a bit possessively through his elbow as we walked toward the entrance, passing under the neon pink sign that I knew so well - the outline of a pink kitten on two legs twirling around a stripper pole.

Underneath the kitten was a list of special events taking place that week: Porn star Dusty Bottom would be appearing on Tuesday, the Breasts & Thighs Chicken Dinner Special was on Wednesday - except somebody had misspelled it "Beasts and Thighs" - and Thursdays were amateur night.

"You think if I flash this we'll get in for free?" I asked.

Chris looked at me with raised eyebrows and let out a whistle.

"Not *these*," I laughed. "*This*." I jingled my pink plastic Jiggly Kitty keychain/bottle opener in his face. Rob Dorfman had given them to our entire office last Christmas. "Nothing says V.I.P. like a free keychain."

"Well in that case, I'm thinking no," said Chris. "But feel free to try."

I took one look at the doorman and put my keychain back in my purse. We paid the cover charge and pushed through the tinted double doors where two more dancing kittens were etched into the glass. I scanned the club for Kendra, but it was hard to see faces through the neon pink glow and the fog machines.

A hostess decked out in pink kitten ears led us to a table close to the stage. After we were seated I tried calling Kendra's cell phone, but she didn't pick up. I was starting to get annoyed, I mean, what the heck was so important that we had to come here? Chris and I ordered two beers from a waitress who was also wearing kitten ears. When she turned to walk back to the bar, a matching pink tail swished enticingly from side to side.

I turned to point this out to Chris, but he was occupied with watching the girl onstage. He wasn't watching her in a lusty, oh-baby, kind of way, rather he was watching her in a 'what-the-fuck is going on?' kind of way. I followed his gaze and am pretty sure that my face morphed into a similar expression, because this girl was truly *awful.* Her moves were stiff, her skin was loose, and she was wobbling like crazy in her six inch clear plastic heels. I saw dimples and stretch marks in places that physicians don't even have names for.

"What the heck is wrong with her?" I asked. She leaned back against the pole to slide down to the floor, but got derailed and fell over backwards. "I thought you had to be fairly decent to get a job here?"

"She's terrible," agreed Chris, watching her with the face of somebody watching open heart surgery on the Discovery Channel. "She should be stripped of her kitten ears."

A man with terrible taste in women eagerly approached the stage and dragged his tinsel stick back and forth. Then he tossed a couple of bills on the floor. The girl knelt down to collect her money and stood back up in the least sexy way possible.

"Can we pay her to *not* take her top off?" I asked.

"Too late," said Chris. "Holy - those things almost hit the floor! Did you see that?"

"I'm trying hard not to," I said, turning my head away and staring at the television over the bar. I always feel sorry for strippers and the fact that they have to pretend to enjoy dancing for creepy and disgusting old men. This particular girl obviously did not belong in the profession, which led me to believe she must be in a pretty dire straits to have ended up here. She walked across the stage to where Chris and I were seated, got down on all fours, and began wagging her finger back and forth in Chris's face. The closer she came the further back he leaned in his chair. If he was wearing a neck tie she might have used it to reel him in.

"Help me," Chris squeaked out of the corner of his mouth.

"Oh man, you're on your own," I said. I pretended to be engrossed in a flyer that was on our table. It had the same information and typos as the sign outside: Dusty Bottom on Tuesday. Beasts & Thighs Chicken Dinner on Wednesday. Amateur night on Thursday. *Thursday.*

"Wow, Chris. Look." I pointed at the flyer. "It's amateur night! That's why this girl sucks!" The stripper gave me a dirty look and retreated to the other side of the stage. *Amateur night. Amateur - Shit!* I put one hand over my mouth and grabbed Chris by the arm with the other.

"She wouldn't," he said, eyes wide, reading my mind.

Before I could answer, the worst stripper in the world finished lapping up her bowl of milk and left the stage. The music changed. An announcer's voice came over the loudspeaker.

"Gentlemen! We have a very special young lady for you tonight. She helped to build The Jiggly Kitty from the bottom up...and now it's our turn to see how she's built from the bottom up!"

"Oh no!" I said, peeking through my fingers. An amused snort escaped from Chris.

"Put your hands together for our naughty engineer - Kendra!"

25

Oh fuck.

The pink curtain at the end of the stage flew open and there she was, wearing nothing but a red lace bra and panties, kitten ears, and a smile that told me instantly she was not in her right mind. Her long blonde hair was twisted into unkempt waves and she strutted down the runway in perfect time to the music, looking every bit the stripper. If she wasn't my boss, and I wasn't completely humiliated, I would have been somewhat impressed.

"She doesn't look half bad up there," said Chris, cocking his head to the side. "But why the heck would she want us to come see this?"

"Oh my God, she must be drunk. Something bad must have happened with Todd!" I stood up to go yank her off the stage, but Chris pulled me back down.

"You can't just climb up there! They'll throw you out of here."

"Well I can't let her take her clothes off!" Why was he so

calm? I was in a panic - waving my arms back and forth trying to get her attention and hissing her name.

"Kendra!" Nothing.

"Kendra!" Louder. Finally she came close enough to make eye contact.

"What the hell are you doing?" I shouted up to her. She did a seductive little wiggle down to the floor so that she was now on her knees in front of Chris, who had an obnoxiously goofy grin on his face. Was I seriously dating this guy?

"Hey," I snapped my fingers. "Over here, look at me." I was less comfortable with Chris looking at Kendra in her underwear than I was with him looking at the last disaster. "What the hell are you doing?"

"I do my little turn on the catwalk! Yeah on the catwalk yeah!" She shouted the words into my face and let out the weirdest laugh I've ever heard. Here I was trying to have a serious conversation and she was singing me a goddamned Right Said Fred song. True to the lyrics she did a little turn at the end of the stage, tossed her hair over her shoulder, and took a couple of graceful spins around the stripper pole. What the hell happened to the MTV-imitating klutz I once knew?

"You think she could teach you this stuff?" asked Chris.

I shot him a dirty look just as the genius in charge of Jiggly Kitty lighting operations decided to turn on the strobes, so that when Kendra unhooked her bra it seemed to be happening in slow motion. I watched in horror as she shrugged off each strap, one frame at a time, and the red lace came sailing through the air, twisting and turning, until coming to rest smack dab on my boyfriend's forehead. I snatched it off of his head and was about to get up on stage whether he liked it or not, when a sight from across the room made me freeze, and then sink slowly back into my seat.

A group of three women and five men, all dressed in business attire, had entered the club and were making their way towards us. The leader of the pack motioned to the walls and the tables, seeming to give some kind of guided tour, though by the body language of two of the women they were not particularly enjoying themselves.

They stepped gingerly and whispered to each other, reeling back at the sight of scantily clad waitresses as if they had walked in on the scene of a bloody massacre. The third woman though, she was in her mid-seventies, wearing a cardigan sweater and a pearl necklace. And she seemed to be enjoying herself immensely. She removed the hostess's kitten ears and tried them on her head - two triangles poked up from between puffs of vibrant orange hair.

I watched this group through the dim lights of the club, unable to make out faces and unable to place the feeling of dread that was quickly growing in the pit of my stomach. They gathered around the opposite side of the stage where I could read their pink V.I.P. badges. They were now close enough for me to see Rob Dorfman's rosy cheeked face harden into a look of shock and anger as it focused squarely on a very topless Kendra. His icy blue eyes met mine as he peeled them off my boss and noticed me there on the opposite side of the stage, looking every bit the idiot assistant. For all he knew, Kendra and I had planned this night together and I was planning to get up there next.

Oh my God oh my God oh my God!

My jaw dropped as the rest of the group fell into place - there was Jasper Quick to his right, the elderly Beatrice Miller in her cardigan and kitty ears to his left, and the rest of the entire Riverlin Zoning Commission lined up behind him, all peering inquisitively up at the stage. They looked up at Kendra who was still oblivious to the fact that the end of the world was happening. She moved to the edge of the stage, bent forward directly in front of Rob, and whipped her hair around in wide circles. I couldn't watch for a second longer.

I hoisted myself up onto the stage and grabbed Kendra around the shoulders. Chris did not try to stop me. He had entered his own state of shock when he realized what was going on and had slid down about twelve inches in his chair. I tried to drag Kendra back toward the curtain, or at least face her away from the crowd, but she seemed to think I had gone up there to dance.

"Whoooo!" she yelled. "Yeah, Tessa! Take it off!" She pulled the left side of my shirt down my shoulder, nearly ripping it. I jerked my arm away.

"No, you idiot!" I screamed into her ear. "Rob is here!" But she wasn't listening. "Rob *Dorfman* is *here*!" I spun her around to face him, pointed, then spun her quickly around again. Recognition finally registered on her face and she clapped one hand over her mouth and the other across her chest. By this point the house lights had come up and security was swarming the stage.

"Ma'am, we need you to step away from the dancer," said a security guard walking towards me slowly as if I were holding Kendra hostage. God he was huge. Another guard snuck up from behind and grabbed me around the neck.

"Hey!" shouted Chris, jumping onto the stage like Batman. "Get your hands off of her!" The first security guard pulled his gun from his holster and aimed it straight at Chris.

Well, this is it Tessa. You finally meet a nice guy and he's about to be shot dead at a Vegas strip club. Mom and Dad will be so proud.

"Sir, you need to step down from the stage immediately!" shouted the guard.

"Whoa!" Chris threw his hands up into the air and looked at me.

"It's okay, just go! I'll be right behind you," I said from the depths of the security guard's armpit. His uniform reeked of perfume and cigarettes, though his armpit smelled surprisingly pleasant. Old Spice. If my neck were to suddenly snap, at least the last thing I smelled wouldn't be body odor. Not that I thought he was going to snap my neck on purpose or anything, but he definitely could have by accident because he was so big and my neck was suddenly feeling like a cheap Jiggly Kitty swizzle stick.

Chris retreated back down the steps followed by the guard with the gun. The guard, being three times Chris's size, merely grabbed him by the wrist and removed him from the club like a child dragging a teddy bear. I followed behind, bent forward and still in a headlock, as if my skull was about to be used as a battering ram. I wasn't sure what happened to Kendra.

"Aren't you going to do anything?" yelled Chris as we passed by Rob. "You're the owner of this damn place! Tell them who we are!"

Rob did not reply. He just watched both of us pass and then thanked the guards for their assistance. The last thing I heard before being shoved out the door was Rob reassuring the Zoning Commission that this type of thing was not typical. I glanced back to see six heads shaking in disapproval. Jasper Quick just smiled.

***

Chris and I were literally thrown out the back door by the dumpsters, just like in the movies.

"I can't believe he let them do this to us!" I said as the door slammed behind me. The muffled sounds of techno music resumed almost immediately.

"I can't believe Kendra just stripped naked in front of one of our biggest clients," said Chris. "Are you okay?"

"I'm fine. You're the one who just had a gun pulled on them! Holy shit." I was half laughing, half in shock, as I straightened out my clothes. It was slowly starting to sink in that this was probably one of those nights you remember forever.

"Let's get the hell out of here," said Chris.

"No, we can't! What about Kendra? Did you see where she went?" I couldn't just leave her there, especially if she was as drunk as I knew she was.

"She ran backstage while Goliath was getting you into that headlock," said Chris, massaging my neck. "You sure you're okay?"

"Fine, I swear." I ran my hand nervously through my hair and looked toward the street, as if I expected to see Kendra drive by topless and blasting I'm Too Sexy from the car stereo. I shook the image from my head. "I hope she didn't try to drive." I tried her cell phone, but there was no answer.

"Come on, let's go see if her car's still here."

Chris and I had almost rounded the corner of the building when the back door to the club swung open again and out stepped Rob Dorfman. I wanted to keep going. I wanted to just get in the car and get the hell out of there as Chris had originally suggested, but this time it was Chris who stopped us in our tracks. He turned and dragged me by the hand back towards Rob, as Rob walked slowly towards us. Any second now Rob would pull a six shooter from his hip and shoot us both dead. I could see it quite clearly, Chris and I being murdered and thrown into a dumpster. I would not have put it past him. But, scared and angry as I was, I knew that Kendra would need me to do damage control. At least as much damage control as was possible under such circumstances.

"Rob, Mr. Dorfman," I said. "what you just saw in there, Kendra's not being herself tonight. She's going through a really tough time, and she, *we,* are horribly, terribly, embarrassed. Please understand."

I still had hope that he would take pity on us. He had known Kendra for years, he would realize that there was obviously something wrong with her, beyond what he normally thought was wrong with her, I mean. And me, the hapless assistant, he would realize that I had been summoned here, unaware, and had tried to stop this. Yes, Rob Dorfman was a human being after all, and he would see everything for what it was.

Boy was I delusional.

The muscles in Rob's jaw tightened as he looked from me to Chris and back again. I could almost hear his teeth grinding.

"I *pay* you people," said Rob, "to make my club look good.

To make it look *respectable* in a business that is not respectable in the least." He pulled a pack of cigarettes from his pocket and lit one up, pacing. "I spend thousands of dollars trying to convince assholes like the ones inside that The Jiggly Kitty is the kind of place that they should *want* to have in their town, that we're *different*." He came around from behind and stood between us, breathing down our necks. "I thought I could at least count on my engineering team to have a little bit of class."

"Mr. Dorfman I'm -" I tried to speak.

"Do you know why I came here tonight?" interrupted Rob, blowing smoke into my face.

"Not really, since you own the place," said Chris. "But I'm a little curious as to why *Beatrice Miller* came here tonight." He took a step to his left and repositioned himself to face Rob. He yanked me by the hand and I joined him.

"I'll tell you why," said Rob. "Despite the fine work your trashy little boss did with Jasper Quick the other night, he was still unable to sway the rest of the Commission."

"Don't you talk about her like that!" I said. "Who's sick idea was that in the first place?" God I hated him.

He ignored me and continued. "My application was going to get denied, and that, that is unacceptable." He ground his cigarette out under his foot. I watched, feeling sick, as if he were grinding Chris and I into the dirt as well. "So I was forced to make a small contribution to the City of Riverlin, in order to help things along."

"So you bribed the entire Zoning Commission?" asked Chris.

"I said I made a *contribution*," said Rob"like I've done a

thousand times before. Only that idiot Beatrice Miller got it into her head that she needed to see the place in person before giving her final vote. Then of course they *all* had to come." He shook his head in disgust.

I nearly laughed out loud when I pictured Beatrice Miller convincing the Zoning Commission that they needed to take a little field trip. That is, until I remembered that if she hadn't insisted on the tour, none of us would be in this mess. I joined Rob in shaking my head in disgust - maybe there was some camaraderie forming here. Maybe Rob would forgive Kendra and instead focusing on hating Beatrice Miller! Hey, it could happen.

"I would have had them. I *had* them," continued Rob, jabbing his index finger in our faces. "Until they spotted that slut up there making her damn stripping debut! What the hell was she doing?"

"I don't know!" I kept repeating. Apparently our alliance against Beatrice Miller wasn't going to work out after all. Then a genius thought dawned on me. "Hey, maybe they didn't even recognize her!" I said.

"You think *Jasper Quick* didn't recognize her? Give me a break! Not only is Jasper inside right now telling everybody exactly who she is, but word is going to spread like wildfire to every other city in Nevada. How many prudish old bats are going to be jumping to approve my applications once they find out what a whore I have representing me?"

I don't know if he had been preparing for a while, or if it was a spur of the moment decision, but the next thing I knew the blur of Chris's right arm came sailing past my left cheek as he punched Rob directly in the nose. Rob went down to the pavement like a ton of bricks, blood everywhere.

"You know," said Chris, for once looking down on the mighty Rob Dorfman, "for the owner of this place, you sure judge the people who choose to work here."

I thought for sure there would be an all out death match as soon as Rob stood up. I imagined myself kneeling over Chris's lifeless body as he lay bleeding in the alley, rain suddenly pouring from the desert sky, the sound of sirens wailing in the distance. But he didn't lunge for Chris or make any attempt to fight back at all. He merely stood up, rather shakily to tell you the truth, and walked backwards to the door of the club, wiping the blood from his face with one hand, and pointing his finger at us with the other.

"Tell your little boss that I'm pulling all my business from your firm, and I mean from *all* branches. We're done." He wrenched open the door and slammed it shut behind him.

26

Chris and I stood in silence for a few seconds.

"Oh my God," I said. "That was so great!" I threw my arms around his neck. "Too bad Kendra didn't get to see that!" What a chivalrous guy he was turning out to be. Despite the fact that I had just witnessed Flamhauser-Geist lose one of its biggest clients, I could barely control my glee. None of that mattered at the moment. Chris had just punched the biggest asshole I've ever known square in the face, and it will forever be the most awesome thing I've ever seen.

The sound of rustling from the far side of one of the dumpsters startled me and brought me back to my senses. I grabbed Chris's arm as I expected to see a rabid raccoon or maybe a hobo lumber out from the trash bags. Instead, Kendra's blonde head peeked around the corner, black mascara running down her cheeks. She was wrapped in a huge flannel shirt with a mysterious oatmeal colored stain down the front.

"There you are!" I ran over and gingerly sat down on the pavement next to her. "You've been back here this whole time?" I asked.

She nodded. "I ran out to go to my car, but I had to puke." She pointed to a spot about three inches away from where I had sat down - oatmeal colored. "Then I heard you guys come out so I just stayed here. I couldn't face Rob again." She rested her head on her knees. "What have I done?" The nights events seemed to have quickly sobered her up.

"It's okay," I said, putting my arm around her. Chris came over to try to comfort her as well, but she burst into fresh tears at the sight of him.

"If you hadn't just seen me naked, I would give you a big hug right now," said Kendra. "I didn't deserve you defending my honor like that. But, thank you."

"It was nothing," said Chris. "And, as far as the whole nudity thing, you have *nothing* to be ashamed of."

I rolled my eyes at him and he quickly retreated to the other side of the dumpster.

"Ken," I said. "Why, *why,* did you do this? What the heck is going on with you?"

"Todd," she said quietly.

"Ah, I figured."

"I ran into the both of them today. Him *and* Carlotta. At Wal-Mart."

"You went into a Wal-Mart?"

"I know right, what are the odds? But I was there, and so were they." She wiped her nose on her sleeve. "And Carlotta is about sixteen years old, I swear, with boobs out to here." She held her arms out about two feet from her body.

"They're probably fake," I said.

"I don't think so," said Kendra. "You know why?" I shook my head. "Because she's seven months pregnant."

My jaw dropped. "Oh Ken, I'm so sorry!"

"I've been ready to have kids for years now!" she said. "But not Todd. No, he was too focused on his *career*. His career! I'm the one running the whole branch! If I didn't think having a baby would ruin *my* career, then he would've been just fine in his cushy little job that my dad set up for him. Director of Business Development. Please! All the stupid ass did was go out drinking and hand out a few business cards. But I went along with what he wanted. Now I'm old, dried up -" she ticked the items off on her fingers, "- I probably killed off any remaining eggs that I had with all the vodka I've been drinking, and it turns out that Todd just didn't want to have kids with *me*."

"Oh please," I said. "I'm sure he didn't plan it! He's probably devastated, I mean his fun-time girlfriend just became more serious than his wife ever was, right?"

"Thanks for trying, Tessa," said Kendra. "But I saw them, and they were having a grand old time. They were in the baby aisle picking out strollers." She closed her eyes and shook her head. "Fucking strollers."

"So what happened, did they see you?" I asked, trying to move on from the subject of strollers.

"Oh they saw me. I kind of snapped and made a huge scene in the middle of Wal-Mart. I'm surprised Jerry Springer didn't swoop in and sign me up for the show. Oh gross!" She finally noticed the puke stain on her shirt and started trying to clean it with her sleeve.

"Here, let me," I said. I mopped it up with a Jiggly Kitty cocktail napkin that was on the ground. Very apropos.

"Then I slapped Todd in the face," said Kendra. "Then I got myself escorted out by Wal-Mart security, about the same way you guys were just escorted out of here. It's really been quiet a day hasn't it?"

"You slapped him?" I asked, smiling. This was turning out to be quite a day indeed. "That's so great."

"It did feel pretty good." She let out a huge sigh. "That is until I got home to my huge, empty, childless, house. I just felt so old and gross, Tessa. You wouldn't understand, you've got your whole life ahead of you."

"We're like four years apart."

Kendra ignored me. "So, I got really drunk, and then I remembered that Thursday nights are amateur night." She put her face in her hands and moaned. "I don't know what I was thinking."

I tossed a pebble back and forth between my hands, thinking back through all the psychology classes I had in college. "You know those criminals," I said finally, "who do something really stupid because deep down they *want* to get caught?"

"Mmm hmmm."

"Well, I think maybe you just really wanted an out. And maybe all this stuff with Todd just gave you a good excuse to go off the deep end. Take the plunge, if you will." I did air quotes around "take the plunge."

"You are so wise and lame for an admin," she laughed.

"Thank you. By the way, where's Bryce tonight?" I asked.

"Dental convention with his buddy."

Ah, Tooth Model. He would have quite enjoyed all this had he been here tonight. Shame.

"Well, everything will turn out okay," I said. "It's not even that bad, it's just one stupid client. We'll be better off without psycho Rob Dorfman terrorizing us anyway. We should all bow down and *thank* you for this, really. My dad always said - "

"Oh God, don't remind me about my dad! He's going to disown me!" Kendra let out a wail of despair and flopped back into a pile of trash bags. "I've disgraced my entire family."

I lied and told her that it wasn't as bad as it seemed, though I couldn't imagine facing *my* dad after a night like this. We sat there for a few more minutes until a car rounded the corner of the building, blinding us with its headlights. Chris had gone and brought the car around. He was turning out to be quite the gentleman, even though he *did* look after he promised not to. I suppose that can be forgiven.

"Come on," I said, standing up and holding out my hand. "Let's get you out of here. We'll sort everything out in the morning."

***

Later that night, after Chris and I had put Kendra to bed, we sat out on her deck drinking gin and tonics with little umbrellas in them that I had found in the kitchen - my feeble attempt at cheering up a miserable evening. There was little doubt in our minds that Chris would find himself unemployed come tomorrow morning. And Kendra's fate was questionable, as was my own.

"I might actually miss Flamhauser-Geist, you know?" said Chris as I snuggled in closer to him on the loveseat. "Kendra and I have worked together for a really long time."

He told me, as he tipped back the last of his drink, that watching me pull Kendra from a pile of trash bags, in a parking lot they had once designed together, was probably the saddest thing he had ever seen.

27

Walking through the office, I did not make eye contact with a single person on Friday morning. Even though I was ninety-nine percent sure that there was no way anybody could have found out about what happened last night, that one percent was enough to make me keep my head down.

I mean, what if it made the eleven o'clock news? What if Roberta Mallard had been sitting on her couch, stuffing her face with a bag of Doritos, and there on the television was a shot of Chris and I being led out of The Jiggly Kitty practically in handcuffs? And then, what if the camera panned over and there was Kendra, whipping her hair around with two blurry boxes over her chest? I couldn't bear it. I particularly wouldn't be able to bear the delight in all my female coworker's eyes when they realized what an absolutely delicious mess Kendra had made of everything.

I bolted to my office, closed the door, and had barely breathed a sigh of relief when the sight of the blinking red message light on my phone gave me about four heart attacks. Nobody ever left messages on my office phone. Nobody except for, maybe, Sean Flamhauser? Or Rob Dorfman? Or

Rob Dorfman's attorney?

Relax! You didn't even do anything wrong! If Rob's attorney is going to call anybody it would be Chris, you know, the guy who punched him? Not that I wished Rob's attorney would call Chris or anything, but the rationalization made me feel a bit better as I dialed into my voicemail. I relaxed at the sound of Kendra's voice. She called in early to tell me that she had been summoned by her father to the Flamhauser compound in Miami Beach.

"Don't even think for a second that I'm going to let you or Chris take any blame for what happened," she tried to reassure me. But her voice lacked confidence, and Chris and I spent the rest of the day jumping every time the phone rang. By the time five o'clock rolled around we had still not heard a peep from either Kendra or her father, and were left with the unknown hanging over our heads for the entire weekend.

On Monday morning I was not only worried about me and Chris, but I was also beginning to get a bit worried about Kendra. I hadn't heard a word from her all weekend - she didn't answer any of my calls or return any of my emails. I was becoming highly suspicious that her father had gone completely nuts and locked her up in some kind of Flamhauser family dungeon set aside for thieves and family members who wished to leave the engineering profession. So I was more than a little relieved when I pulled into the parking lot after lunch and saw the familiar blue BMW parked once again in its reserved spot.

I practically ran up to the office, but stopped short outside of Kendra's door as my stomach did a few nervous back flips. This was it! By this time tomorrow I could very well be on a plane back to Massachusetts, no longer an employee of Flamhauser-Geist. I imagined myself sneaking into the office to pack up my things and bumping into Nick, or worse yet, my boss Tom Skeeter. I would have to explain to him how in a few short months I had contributed to my entire team being fired, and how I was involved in the biggest scandal ever to hit Flamhauser-Geist. I never in my wildest dreams could have imagined my boring administrative career ending in such a way. Tom's bouncy curls would probably keel over and die when they heard the news. God I would feel terrible.

I knocked timidly on Kendra's door and poked my head inside. There in front of me was not the typical boss I was used to greeting on Monday morning. She was not spread out on the floor working on plans, or barking orders into the phone wearing one expensive suit or another. But she was not the new Kendra that I expected to see either - tear-streaked and depressed, lamenting her mistakes. No, this was a third Kendra, one dressed in jeans and a t-shirt, hair in a ponytail, looking rather relaxed and happy. She was, however, packing.

"Hey you," the third Kendra said, smiling at me over her shoulder as she removed a painting from the wall.

"Hey," I said. I glanced around the office and my face fell as I took in the number of cardboard boxes everywhere. "You're packing."

"That is correct," she said, wrapping the painting in newspaper and adding it to one of the boxes. "I would have called you but I got in really late last night. It was just so relaxing down there. I didn't want to leave, you know?"

I didn't quite know. Relaxing wasn't something I'd experienced in quite some time. I sat down on the white leather couch and watched her putter around. "Um, so you got disowned and fired, yet you had a really nice weekend?" I asked. "Stop packing for a sec and come talk to me."

Kendra stopped what she was doing and sat down behind her desk, mostly hidden behind packing boxes. "He's my dad," she said. "He didn't fire me."

"But you're packing," I repeated.

"Well, he didn't fire me, but he strongly suggested that I voluntarily step down from my position." She could barely keep the smile off of her face. "I tell you, Tessa, as soon as he said those words to me everything I've been bottling up all these years just came pouring out. I told him how unhappy I am being an engineer, and how I wished I had never let him and mom convince me to give up art. And for once he actually listened!" She spun around in her chair to face the wall of windows overlooking The Strip. "There was just something about his little girl getting up on stage at The Jiggly Kitty that made him open his eyes."

"That'll do it," I said.

She spun back around to face me. "I just feel like maybe this whole thing with Todd leaving, and with Jasper Quick, maybe it was all leading to this. Maybe it was supposed to happen this way. Maybe this was my only way out, I don't know. But I just feel so relieved, so ready for what's next!"

"That's awesome," I said, wishing she would hurry up and inform the rest of us of what was next. "I was really worried about you this weekend - Chris and I both were. Well, when we weren't working on his resume -"

"Oh, I'm so sorry Tessa, I should have called you guys about that! Tell Chris not to worry for even a second longer! My dad knows he was only defending me when he punched

Rob. And he also knows *everything* about Rob."

"Everything?" I asked, thinking of his little match-making scheme with Jasper.

"*Everything,*" said Kendra. "I had to tell him, I mean he was dialing the number to give Chris his walking papers when I blurted it all out." She buried her face in her hands and shook her head back and forth. "Believe me, I never want to have that conversation with my dad ever again. But it was a necessary evil."

I cringed at the thought. "You're a brave girl, Kendra Stoltz."

"*Flamhauser,*" Kendra corrected me.

"Ah, Kendra *Flamhauser*, sorry." I smiled at this reinvented Kendra Flamhauser in her Mickey Mouse t-shirt, who suddenly looked ten years younger. "Chris will be very happy to hear what you did."

"But I didn't even tell you the best part yet! As soon as I told him everything, my dad got on the phone, called Rob, and told him *exactly* what he thought of him! I have never heard so many swear words come out of my dad's mouth, Tessa. It was incredible! I wish I had taken a video and put it up on YouTube. I mean, anybody who has ever dealt with Rob Dorfman would die to have witnessed what I did."

I was truly happy for her, I really was. I was ecstatic that Rob Dorfman had gotten what he deserved. And I was thrilled that Kendra was getting out of the business that had made her so unhappy. But a small, jealous, part of me that I don't like to acknowledge was suddenly fighting back tears. Kendra was going to go off and fulfill her dreams of becoming an artist and I would be stuck here, or worse yet, stuck in freezing cold Massachusetts, forever typing letters and sending faxes. Where was *my* way out? Son of a -

"So, what now?" I asked, plastering a smile back onto my face.

"Well," said Kendra, "I actually have a little surprise for you."

"For me?" I brightened up a bit.

"Yes for you!" She was still beaming. "Hold on." She leaned down, pulled a three ring binder from her purse, and plunked it down in front of me. The words *Golden Opportunity, LLC* were printed on the cover over a logo of two long-haired heads with a martini glass between them. "You've been such a good friend to me, Tess. I mean, since the moment I met you at the Christmas party and through all my meltdowns these past few months, you've been nothing but wonderful. So I wanted to do something for you, for me too, but mostly for you. You deserve a chance to get out of here."

A chance to get out of here. My heart beat a little quicker as I opened the cover of the binder.

Mission Statement of Golden Opportunity, LLC

"I thought you'd get a kick out of the name," said Kendra, watching me intently as I continued to read.

To provide joy to the dwellers of offices, nursing homes, hospitals, detention centers, and other creatively restrictive facilities, through art lessons, projects, and the encouragement to discover and embrace their artistic talents.

"So what do you think?" she asked. "I ran it past my dad and he's willing to help us out financially at first - keep us on the Flamhauser payroll until we get going. Parents are cool sometimes." She watched my face for a reaction, but I was in shock. I flipped through page after page of research that she had done on opening a small business, and the pages of ideas she had for potential clients and projects. No wonder she didn't have time to call me.

"Are you sure you want to do this?" I asked, finally looking up at her. "I mean, with me?"

"Come on, Tessa, who else? Rob Dorfman? I said that everything happened for a reason, didn't I? So don't tell me that a fellow art lover landing herself in Las Vegas, equally miserable with her job, wasn't fate."

"Hmm," I said, rolling my eyes. "I think somebody else may have mentioned that once before."

"Yeah, yeah," said Kendra. "I'm sorry about that, I just wasn't quite ready back then. But I'm ready now. This is all, of course, assuming you were planning to stay here in Vegas. With you and Chris, I just kind of figured -"

"I'm staying," I interrupted, more certain of it now than ever. "I'm staying."

Kendra clapped her hands and gave an excited little bounce in her chair. She spun around again to look out the windows.

"I'm sure going to miss this view though," she said.

"I'm going to miss boots."

"Boots?"

"Winter boots," I said. "And sweaters. And maybe even snow, but just a little bit."

"You can still wear boots," she said. "I saw a guy this

morning wearing plastic rain boots, a mini skirt, and a coconut bra. Swear to God. Anything goes around here."

"True," I laughed. "What's not to love about this city?"

"Let's not waste another minute then, shall we?"

Kendra reached through the narrow space between two boxes, and we shook on the deal.

EPILOGUE

"Do you find it ironic, at all," said Chris, pouring us two glasses of champagne, "that we're celebrating our anniversary by watching something collapse?"

We were relaxing in our hotel suite, preparing to watch the implosion of a neighboring hotel at 2:30 in the morning. It also happened to be the one year anniversary of the day that Chris and I met, and a much needed break from my relentless wedding planning. Yes, you heard me correctly. On my fantastically *last* day of work as an administrative assistant, Chris asked me to marry him.

Well, to be completely accurate, first he asked me to fetch him a file. I called him quite a few names in my head as I walked to the filing cabinets that morning. I mean, I love the guy and all, but that one last act of administrative slavery really ticked me off. He should have brought me flowers, or some kind of departing gift, not sent me off on an assignment! Did something happen to his legs that I did not know about?

Of course it was then, as I angrily wrenched the file from the drawer, that I found the most beautiful 3/4 carat diamond ring tied to the front of the folder with a note attached asking me to turn around. I followed the instructions, only to find the nerd already down on one knee behind me. A thousand heads popped out of their cubicles to see what was going on. And that was it.

He asked me right there, in front of all of our coworkers and one amused photocopier repairman. True, we had only been dating a matter of months, but when you know you know. No additional amount of months or years was necessary to confirm that with Chris, I knew. And if there is a city in the world notorious for marrying somebody you haven't known very long, well, we were in it.

"No, it's perfect," I said from my chair by the window. With my feet up on the radiator I watched his reflection in the glass as he walked toward me. "Could you turn off the lamp?" Our reflections disappeared with a flick of the switch, and then nothing but night sky and the bright lights of Vegas lay before us.

Chris still works at Flamhauser-Geist. And when Kendra stepped down, Tom Skeeter, with his personnel file full of rejected Vegas transfer requests, was offered her position. Let's just say that Sean Flamhauser felt he owed me a small favor for sticking by his daughter.

Loose Cannons took over as one of Flamhauser-Geist's biggest clients, and lucky for Chris, Dan, and the rest of the team, Jimmy Cannon turned out to be one of the nicest people on the face of the earth. The only downside was that Tom Skeeter frowned upon playing video games in the office, forcing Chris and Dan to sell their system and their gaming chairs to a local twelve year old. Though they later agreed that without the constant abuse of Rob Dorfman, the stress relief of Mortal Kombat was virtually unnecessary.

"I'm pretty excited about this," said Chris, settling into the chair beside me. "I've never seen one of these before."

"Me neither. Oh look, there it goes." At precisely 2:30 a.m., with a few flashes of light and a deep rumble, the hotel began to fall.

"Kaboom," said Chris.

"Kaboom."

I watched as the hotel came down from left to right, folding in on itself and forming an enormous cloud of dust and debris that covered our view of the ground. When the dust settles there will be a vacant lot ready and waiting for the construction of something bigger, something better.

Something that maybe, just maybe, nobody ever saw coming.

ABOUT THE AUTHOR

Beth Labonte was born in Salem, Massachusetts and received a B.A. in Sociology from the University of Massachusetts Amherst in 2001. Currently working as an Administrative Assistant, she has taken to writing as her creative outlet in an excruciatingly mundane corporate world.

Beth resides outside of Worcester, Massachusetts, with her husband, son, and two cats.

Visit her website at www.bethlabonte.com

2347111R00147

Printed in Germany
by Amazon Distribution
GmbH, Leipzig